S0-BMU-913

SHOWDOWN IN DEAD'S MAN CANYON

When Rattigan Cooke and his brother Bradley are given the most sought after job at the Silver Creek mine of delivering silver to Bear Rock, their good fortune doesn't last. While making their first delivery, they meet a man who is alone and afoot on the trail.

They take the man to Bear Rock, but they regret their kind act when he reveals that he's the notorious gunslinger Corbin Metz and he steals their silver. The brothers pursue the gunslinger, but their mission soon goes badly wrong. Bradley is crippled in a gunfight with Corbin and Rattigan is jailed for confronting the vicious railroad man Victor Greystone, who wants to find Corbin to protect his own secrets.

With the odds so stacked against them, can the brothers make Corbin regret the day he crossed them?

By the same author

SHOWDOWN IN DEAD MAN'S CANYON

SCOTT CONNOR

CULBIN PRESS

Names, characters and incidents in this book are fictional, and any resemblance to actual events, locales, organizations, or persons living or dead, is purely coincidental.

Copyright © 2013, 2016 by Scott Connor
ISBN: 9798595444927

All rights reserved.
No part of this book may be reproduced, or stored in a retrieval system, or transmitted in any form or by any means, electronic, mechanical, photocopying, recording, or otherwise, without express written permission of the author.

Published by Culbin Press.

PROLOG

"Leave us for a few minutes," Victor Greystone said with an exasperated sigh. "Then these two can sort out their little misunderstanding."

Marshal Ken Dagwood and Corbin Metz sneered at each other, suggesting that even if they were left alone for the rest of the year, they'd still be at loggerheads. So the deputy marshals Eddie Bishop and Richard Crane turned to their boss for guidance.

When he nodded, they left the railroad office, which encouraged the dismissed railroad men to troop out after them. The three men left in the office didn't move until the door downstairs closed.

Then Victor sat on the edge of his desk while Corbin stood by the door. Marshal

Dagwood went to the window that overlooked the town of Bear Rock.

"Perhaps now we're alone, we can stop mincing words," Dagwood said.

"Sure," Corbin said. "This is a railroad town filled with railroad workers. The town marshal should be sympathetic to our concerns."

"Except we know this isn't a dispute about which one of us controls railroad security. It's really about your boss, a man who achieved his position with intimidation and bribes." Dagwood bunched a fist. "I'm the law in Bear Rock and I'm noting everything he says and does. One day soon I'll use it against him."

"As we're talking freely, I'll say that every man has his price. I've yet to find yours."

"You're wrong. You're talking to the only man in town who can't be bought."

Dagwood turned from the window and then flinched. While he and Corbin had been trading taunts, Victor had drawn a six-shooter on him. Dagwood's wide eyes showed he was surprised Victor had dared to act so openly.

He shook his head, seemingly confident that Victor wouldn't carry out his threat, but Victor fired, blasting a deadly shot into the marshal's heart. Dagwood stumbled to the side clutching his chest.

Then he keeled over backward, hitting the window in the center and disappearing from view in a shower of glass. A thud sounded outside as he slammed down on the ground.

"Then we have nothing more to say to each other," Victor said with a smirk. Then he deposited his gun in a drawer and pointed at the door. "The next few hours will be difficult, Corbin. I need help to explain this away."

"I'll round everyone up," the dutiful Corbin said before he hurried from the room.

Corbin took the back stairs so he avoided Bishop and Crane who came hurrying up the main stairs. They burst into the office with guns brandished to find that Victor was standing at the broken window. He didn't appear to register that they had arrived until they joined him at the window.

"What happened?" Deputy Bishop asked.

"The argument between Corbin and our marshal got out of hand so Corbin shot him," Victor said, his voice cracking with emotion. "Then he ran, but you can rest assured that I'll do everything I can to help you bring him to justice."

ONE

"Stop right there," Rattigan Cooke said.

Talbot Court faced Rattigan and snorted with contempt.

"You'll stop me, will you?" he said.

"I will, because you have to listen to me." Rattigan pointed at the miners who had gathered for this confrontation. "You all do."

Talbot tipped back his hat in irritation at Rattigan's attitude, and his expression tightened when from out of the darkness of the tunnel Rattigan's brother Bradley emerged and stood with Rattigan.

"If you don't listen to him, you'll listen to me," Bradley said with a roll of his shoulders.

Despite the mine's enclosed working conditions, the brothers rarely exchanged more than the occasional word so his support was welcome. It also made the miners frown as they weighed up which side of this argument they wanted to be on.

The miners at the Silver Gulch mine were always arguing; the work was hard and there wasn't much entertainment to be had in Silver Creek, but the last week had been more argumentative than usual. A tunnel had collapsed killing two miners, Wilson Thorne and Lloyd Fincher.

This was the first fatal accident in a while and these men had been popular with their enthusiasm providing a calming influence. With that now gone, grumbling discontent had grown and, in the poisonous atmosphere, rumors had gathered credence.

Some said the latest mine owner Frank Johnson was having financial problems and that meant they wouldn't get paid. Some even claimed the accident could be blamed on him. Talbot was the ring-leader of the discontent and he had organized a delegation of miners to gather at sundown in a tunnel to confront Frank. Rattigan had become tired of the unease and he was relieved that he wasn't alone in not agreeing with the complaints.

"So it's two against ten," Talbot said when no more miners joined Rattigan and Bradley.

Bradley took a long pace forward to stand toe to toe with Talbot.

"Yeah," he said. "Do you want to back down now?"

Talbot's answer was to snarl and push Bradley away. Then, with a shoulder down, he charged him, shoving him on into the tunnel wall. With that, Rattigan faced the other men. He'd hoped the rest wouldn't be as angry as Talbot was and he'd get a chance to talk with them rationally, but that possibility died when several men moved in on him at once.

The entrance to the tunnel was twenty feet away and Rattigan turned to it, but before he could move off, they surrounded him. Then they all closed in. Rattigan raised his fists in a futile attempt to defend himself, but within moments he was overwhelmed.

Trapped in a forest of whirling arms he was quickly batted to the ground, although Bradley was faring better than he was. Bradley had already knocked over Talbot, another man was lying on his back and he was wading into the rest of the mob that wasn't attacking him.

Heartened, Rattigan clambered to his feet. He barged one man aside, thumped a second man in the stomach and tripped up a third. He was looking for his next target when a hand slapped down on his shoulder.

Rattigan jerked his elbow backward, but it failed to hit flesh and worse, that gave his assailant the opportunity to grab his arm and yank it up his back. Rattigan squirmed without success until he noticed that the mob had all taken a backward pace and even Bradley had stopped fighting. Frank Johnson's men had arrived.

"You're coming with us," Rattigan's assailant said in his ear.

"This isn't what it seems," Rattigan said.

"They all say that. Save the excuses for Frank."

Rattigan was turned away while two men moved in and secured Bradley. With Talbot and the rest acting with apparent innocence, they were led from the tunnel and across the mine to the tents that housed Frank and the rest of the mine's management.

When one of the guards went inside Frank's tent, Bradley and Rattigan sighed at the irony of being punished for fighting when they'd been defending Frank. After a few minutes, the guard came out and beckoned them to enter.

Nobody followed them in and for one of the rare times since he'd come to work here, Rattigan faced the mine boss. Frank's steely gaze complimented his steel-hair. He was sitting with a turned-over book on his lap and a bottle of liquor at his feet.

"I've been told an interesting story about your exploits tonight," Frank said.

Frank's calm tone, which suggested this meeting might not turn out as badly as he'd feared, made Rattigan relax his stance.

"It wasn't like it seemed," Rattigan said. "We fought with a group of miners who were trying to gather support for their complaints."

"I know. Talbot's been itching to cause trouble since Wilson's and Lloyd's unfortunate deaths." Frank bade them to sit down and he didn't speak again until they'd located chairs and positioned them facing him. "So it must have taken guts to stand up to him alone."

"We're not alone. We all accept that conditions here are tough, but it just needs men like Talbot to gather support and those grievances build."

"Then we're of the same mind, and I like that." Frank gave a benign smile and then turned to Bradley for his view.

"I agree with most of what Talbot says, but not with the way he planned to raise his concerns," Bradley said, making Frank raise an eyebrow in surprise.

"I also like men who speak their mind, and I want to make conditions safer, too. I'll call a meeting before the first shift tomorrow and deal with the matter." Frank spread his hands, inviting them to say more, but with this encounter having gone better than either man could have expected, they said nothing. "Although you might not be around to attend."

"Why?" Bradley and Rattigan said together.

"Your behavior tells me that I can trust you, and I rarely meet miners I can trust unconditionally. The last two were Wilson and Lloyd."

For several seconds silence reigned as the brothers digested that information.

"You want us to fetch supplies?" Rattigan said hopefully, his guess making Bradley beam at the possibility that Frank might be about to offer them one of the few desirable jobs at the mine.

"That's my offer." Frank waited while both men punched the air with delight. "Wilson and Lloyd would have made the trip to Bear Rock tomorrow, but last week's sad events mean I have an opening. I assume you're interested?"

The railroad was building a track to the mine, but with that work incomplete, supplies had to be brought in from Bear Rock. The three-week round trip was fraught with dangers from the unforgiving terrain and from the bandits that sometimes ventured into the area, but as an alternative to spending all day underground, the trip was Rattigan's idea of heaven. Although, as a long trip with only his argumentative brother for company was his idea of hell, he checked that Bradley was smiling as widely as he was, and he received an eager nod.

"We sure are," Rattigan said.

"I'm pleased." Frank tapped his fingers together, his pursed lips promising them that despite the welcome offer, there was a less appealing element. "There's one other matter that I entrusted to Wilson and Lloyd, and which they kept secret. I expect the same discretion from you."

"Of course," Bradley said.

"So as not to draw unwanted attention, when supplies come in, I deliver batches of silver to Bear Rock. You'll take around twenty thousand dollars' worth." Frank smiled. "You'll deliver it to Victor Greystone and thankfully he's the most trustworthy man you could ever hope to meet."

Rattigan shrugged. "We didn't know about that, but if the shipment is a secret, that shouldn't make the trip any harder."

"It shouldn't, but the other rumor Talbot spread is true. I have financial problems, so I can't afford for the shipment to be stolen." Frank narrowed his eyes, his expression grave. "So take no chances and, if you lose the silver, don't come back!"

TWO

"Keep going," Bradley said. "That man looks like trouble."

On the seat of the covered wagon, Rattigan frowned.

"He's not packing a gun," he said.

"I *don't* care about that." Bradley waggled a finger at him. "I *do* care about the coffin!"

The man was standing alone with a saddlebag draped over a shoulder and a foot set on what appeared to be a recently-made coffin. This was the first unusual situation they had encountered after an uneventful journey from Silver Creek.

Mindful of the need to avoid people, they'd steered away from the railroad. So the only settlement they'd passed through had been the burned-out wreck of Red

Creek. They had moved quickly down the short main drag between the rows of broken down and burned buildings.

None of them had showed signs of recent habitation, but when they'd emerged, the lone man had been standing on the trail ahead. Rattigan recalled Frank's last order for them to take no chances and he agreed with Bradley about the need for caution, but after a ten-day journey that had been a quiet and strained ordeal for both men, he welcomed talking with someone else. So he drew back on the reins and stopped the wagon a dozen yards on from the lone man.

"I'm Corbin," the man declared when he'd hurried on to meet them.

"What are you doing out here all alone with a coffin, Corbin?" Bradley said before Rattigan could reply, his low tone hinting that only a good answer would result in him being allowed to ride with them.

"It's an empty coffin and a long story," Corbin said with a lively tone that said they'd only get to hear that story if they let him ride along.

"That's a pity. We haven't got the time to wait for it."

Bradley lunged for the reins forcing Rattigan to draw them away and making Corbin frown.

"The coffin is a personal matter, and I'm heading to Bear Rock," he said quickly. "My brother Delano lives there, but ten miles out of Red Creek my wagon wheel broke and my horse keeled over. I reckon I will, too, if you leave me afoot."

Rattigan nodded and patted the seat beside him, and Bradley's only objection was to mutter under his breath about how Corbin's woes weren't his problem. With a relieved sigh Corbin hurried back to the coffin while Rattigan jumped down.

Mindful of Corbin's comment that the matter was personal he didn't help him move the coffin. Instead, he lowered the tailboard and shoved items aside to clear a space behind the covered crates in which the silver had been stored.

Corbin slipped the coffin into the freed space. When he deposited the saddlebag inside, Rattigan noticed the plaque on the lid. It held an inscription headed up by initials that, upside down, looked like KD, which meant nothing to him.

Corbin acknowledged that Rattigan had seen the plaque by smiling before he turned away. When they'd both rejoined Bradley, he said nothing for a while as Rattigan moved the wagon on, tracking alongside the dry creek that had given the town its name.

"If you headed to that ghost town, you can't have been this way for a while," Rattigan prompted.

"I often come here," Corbin said, his tone troubled. "I used to live in Red Creek back in the days when you miners passed through regularly."

Bradley stiffened, but then he snorted a laugh as he accepted that their blackened clothes and the fact that they were heading away from Silver Creek meant that knowing their identities wasn't suspicious.

"We didn't know they used this route," Rattigan said. "This is our first trip out for supplies."

Corbin winked. "Does that mean Wilson Thorne and Lloyd Fincher aren't taking out the silver shipments no more?"

Rattigan winced while beside him Bradley tensed.

"They died," Rattigan said levelly.

Corbin gave a sharp intake of breath and then gnawed at his bottom lip, his concerned attitude removing Rattigan's suspicion that his knowledge and question had a sinister intent. Bradley didn't relax and, as they rode beside the creek, he firmed his jaw and muttered to himself. Rattigan judged they were an hour out of Bear Rock when Corbin got their attention and pointed at a formation of boulders.

"My brother lives up in Dead Man's Canyon," he said. "So I'll get off by the boulders."

"We can take you to his house."

"I'd prefer it if you didn't."

Rattigan shrugged and decided not to pry. Bradley even mustered a smile, although presumably that was only because Corbin was leaving them. When they reached the boulders, Rattigan halted the wagon letting Corbin jump down.

Rattling sounded as Corbin moved the coffin, making the suspicious Bradley turn to the back of the wagon, although only the front end of the covered crates was visible. Despite his concern, the crates stayed covered and a minute later Corbin slapped the side of the wagon and hollered that they could leave. Rattigan trundled the wagon on and, after a few minutes, he checked behind them, but Corbin had already disappeared from view.

"I still say that was a bad idea," Bradley said.

Rattigan shrugged, not letting his brother's ill-mood dampen his developing good mood.

"What are you planning to do first when we get to town?" he asked.

"The only thing on my mind is getting this shipment handed over to Victor Greystone."

"I agree, but it's been six months since I last spent time in a big town like Bear Rock." Rattigan sighed. "So first I'm jumping into the hottest, sweetest smelling bath anyone's ever poured. Then I'm finding the biggest and noisiest saloon with the strongest liquor."

Rattigan smiled, but Bradley didn't take the opportunity to lighten his serious demeanor.

"Visiting a town like Bear Rock is what's worrying me the most. So put aside those thoughts and start looking out for trouble or you'll never get a chance to enjoy a bath or a saloon."

Rattigan frowned, but he did as he'd been told. Despite Bradley's concern, on the last leg of the journey, they still didn't pass anybody and, when they approached the first buildings, it looked as if Bradley's fears were misplaced.

They had timed their journey so that they'd arrive on the pre-arranged day at sundown. When the town opened up to them, few people were outside, although these people all watched them.

Rattigan was about to report this observation to Bradley, but he decided not to when he accepted that these men would work for the railroad. Before they'd left Silver Creek, Frank had detailed the hand-over process.

Victor Greystone would sign the paper-work and take the silver into the station house where the railroad men would take up residence. Wilson and Lloyd had never stayed in town for long enough to see what happened when the train arrived, but Victor's unblemished record spoke for itself.

Six riders were lined up in front of the station house so Rattigan swung the wagon round to place it beside the office and facing the station where the riders considered them silently. Their arrogance made Rattigan shuffle on his seat with discomfort, so he turned to the office where a man, presumably Victor Greystone, was standing at an upstairs window.

Victor moved away and two minutes passed in silence until, at an unhurried pace, he came outside. He stopped beside a rider and spoke quietly with him. His comments made that man survey the scene before he nodded.

Then they moved on to the wagon. Clutched under Victor's arm were papers, which he consulted before moving out of view. Bradley and Rattigan both shrugged at his offhand manner before jumping down. They found Victor at the back of the wagon.

"You two are new," he said.

"Wilson and Lloyd died," Rattigan said as Bradley lowered the tailboard.

This comment made Victor frown, breaking him out of his dismissive attitude.

"Gallagher, take over," he said to the other man before he turned to Rattigan. "How?"

"It was in a mine accident. . . ." Rattigan trailed off as Gallagher had seen the coffin lying in the back of the wagon.

Gallagher raised himself and twisted his neck to read the inscription. His eyes opened wide and he dropped back down where he rounded on Bradley.

"What kind of damn fool game are you playing?" he demanded.

"That coffin has nothing to do with us," Bradley said, still shocked that it was somehow still there.

"Then who. . . ?"

Gallagher turned back to the coffin as the lid went hurtling into the air. From within Corbin rose up with a six-shooter in hand and a grin on his face. Victor dove aside, as did Bradley and Rattigan, but Gallagher stayed transfixed.

He paid for his slowness in reacting when two rapid gunshots tore out. Gallagher went staggering backward with his chest holed before tumbling over on to his back. Rattigan took refuge at the side of the wagon with Bradley as the riders and the other men on the main drag reacting in a quick and well-practiced manner.

Men hurried into positions at the corners of buildings on either side of the station house while the riders spread out seeking to surround the wagon. For their part Rattigan and Bradley shrugged at each other as they thought about what they could do.

Bradley fingered his trusty Colt, but Rattigan was unarmed. Then a ferocious burst of gunfire tore out from the back of the wagon. The firing was so rapid Corbin must be using two guns and although it was too wild to hit anyone, the volley forced the riders who were seeking to close in on the wagon to scatter.

As these men took refuge out of the direct line of fire from the back of the wagon, Bradley frowned, accepting he could do little to help other than get caught in the cross-fire. So he and Rattigan hurried to the office and pressed their backs to the wall to await developments.

Thirty seconds passed without further gunfire so Victor barked out an order, dispatching two men to head around to the front of the wagon. They moved cautiously, craning their necks, but when they reached the seat, gunfire cracked and both men went spinning to the ground, their chests bloodied.

As the men became still, another volley of gunfire tore out sending men on the other side of the main drag scurrying into cover. Then Corbin clambered into view on the seat, having made his way along the inside of the wagon.

He took hold of the reins in one hand while training his gun from side to side, seeking out anyone else who was foolish enough to confront him. He treated Rattigan and Bradley to a mocking salute before the wagon moved off.

Then the wagon gathered speed and hurtled out of town heading back along the route they'd taken. As trail dust spiraled into the sky, in short order a ragged bunch of riders launched their pursuit.

"Do you reckon they'll catch him?" Bradley asked as Victor darted about urging the rest of his men to pursue Corbin.

"From the way Corbin was shooting, I hope for their sakes that they don't," Rattigan said.

THREE

"There's not much to your story," Marshal Eddie Bishop said.

"That's because we didn't see much," Rattigan said.

The marshal nodded and turned to the scowling Victor Greystone. It was evening and Bishop had gathered the relevant people in the railroad office. Earlier, he had detailed Corbin Metz's past, confirming it had been a terrible mistake to let him ride with them.

Last year, a consignment of silver had been stolen from the train, so the railroad had hired the gunslinger Corbin. His reputation had resolved most problems without bloodshed, but last month he'd crossed the line when in a dispute over railroad security, he'd killed the previous town marshal.

Since then, he'd been on the run until Rattigan and Bradley had met him. They presumed that after he had gotten off the wagon, he'd sneaked back on board with the coffin and hid inside it.

After stealing the silver shipment, the other railroad men except for Victor had pursued him. Victor's downbeat demeanor while Rattigan had described what had happened showed he didn't think they'd catch him.

"Not seeing much is convenient," Victor said.

"We weren't responsible for what happened," Bradley said, turning to him.

"Then explain why Corbin didn't overcome you at Red Creek and then escape with the silver instead of stealing it in town when he had to shoot up half my men?"

Bradley's eyes blazed, but before he could retort, Marshal Bishop stepped in front of him.

"Quit the accusations," he said. "I reckon you've answered your own question. This was an attack on you, and the silver was a way to get close to you, although I'm sure it was a welcome bonus. In fact, you were lucky you spoke with Rattigan, or you'd have found the coffin first and Corbin would have shot you instead of Gallagher."

Victor nodded. "Because I was the only witness to him killing Marshal Ken Dagwood."

"I understand now," Rattigan said, and then shrugged after drawing everyone's attention to him. "The initials KD were on the coffin."

Marshal Bishop nodded while rubbing his chin as he digested this information, but Victor waved an arm angrily.

"So you two met a gunslinger carrying a coffin inscribed with the initials of the lawman he'd killed, and you brought him into town." He shook his head. "You're either the two most stupid men who've ever lived or—"

Victor didn't get to complete his latest accusation as Bradley stepped around Bishop and launched a scything blow at his cheek that sent him stumbling backward for a pace until he toppled over. Bradley stood over him forcing Bishop to step in and clamp a restraining hand on his shoulder, but Bradley shrugged him off.

"Get up so I can knock you down again," Bradley said.

"Few men have ever dared to hit me. Nobody has ever hit me twice."

Bradley rocked forward, looking as if he might risk being the first, before he shook his head and turned on his heel. With his shoulders hunched he stormed across the office.

"We need to explain ourselves," Rattigan shouted after him.

"You can explain," Bradley said as he disappeared through the door. "I'll be in the Sagebrush saloon."

Rattigan contemplated following him out, but he figured that would only make matters worse and he held out a hand to Victor, who ignored him and stood up on his own.

"I hope you take that outburst into account when you piece together who's to blame for this," Victor said to Bishop.

"I already have and I reckon you got off lightly," Bishop said. "If I'd have been him, I'd have punched you through the wall."

Rattigan hid his smile behind his hand, but Victor paid him no attention as he headed around his desk and sat down heavily.

"These miners are hiding something," he said.

In response Bishop walked back and forth across the office with his head lowered, his silence seemingly designed to lower the tension. Then he leaned back against the wall and spoke to Victor using a soft tone.

"Now that I've heard their version of today's events, tell me your version, from the beginning," he said.

Fifteen minutes later, Rattigan headed out of the office. He found Bradley hunched over at the bar in the Sagebrush saloon, contemplating his whiskey glass as if he might find the answer to his problems there.

"Did it get any better?" Bradley asked.

"Nope. After you left, it got a whole lot worse." Rattigan collected a glass and

Bradley filled it. "The marshal accepts that Corbin acted alone, but Victor's convinced we helped him."

Rattigan sipped his drink, feeling unwilling to complete the story in case Bradley overreacted, but Bradley accepted that revelation with a shrug.

"I'd gathered that much before I hit him."

"Except he then described what happened outside the railroad office and it didn't sound much like the incident we saw." He waved a hand as he struggled to encapsulate the half-truths and interpretations Victor had put on the events. "In short, we distracted him and stopped him noticing Corbin in the back of the wagon until it was too late."

Bradley shrugged. "He must be even more fearful of losing his job than we are."

Rattigan winced. The chaos of the last few hours had stopped him thinking about their employment situation. He swirled his drink and downed it before replying.

"Frank's last words were not to return if we lost the silver, but we still ought to go back and explain what happened."

"I agree, but even if Frank accepts it was the railroad's fault, he won't trust us with making this journey again."

Rattigan nodded. He refilled both their glasses before providing the final piece of bad news.

"Victor says the railroad didn't lose the silver, as Corbin stole it before he took responsibility." Rattigan waited until Bradley's mouth fell open. "In other words, Corbin's raid was the mine's loss, not the railroad's."

Bradley gripped his glass tightly. "Frank won't be able to pay the miners and that could mean the end for the mine."

"If that happens, the miners will tear us apart," Rattigan said unhappily.

"They'll tear *you* apart," Bradley said. "I'm not returning now, and if I ever meet Frank Johnson or any of the miners again, I'll be sure to tell them it was your fault."

"I'm obliged for your support," Rattigan said, but Bradley had already turned his back on him.

SHOWDOWN IN DEAD MAN'S CANYON

* * *

The train was due in an hour and with his limited funds the farthest Rattigan could travel was Fort Riley, the next station along the line. Two days ago, Marshal Bishop had told him to stay in town until he had finished his investigation.

Despite that, Rattigan couldn't afford to stay here for any longer or he'd use up the last of his money. As the railroad men had failed to find Corbin, today he'd accepted that returning to Silver Creek was foolhardy.

With the reputation he was likely to have gathered from his role in the raid, he'd also accepted he wouldn't find work in Bear Rock. He didn't know what Bradley's plans were, as he hadn't seen him since leaving the Sagebrush saloon two nights ago.

Back then, Bradley had been embarking on a mission to drink himself into oblivion. As this would have soured his mood even more, Rattigan had decided that putting some distance between himself and his brother would be better for both of them.

While he waited for the ticket office to open, Rattigan wandered around the station house. He'd taken a single step on to the platform when he came to a sudden halt. Victor Greystone was standing before him.

"You don't leave town until I say you can go," Victor said, taking a long pace forward.

Rattigan struggled to think of an appropriate reply, but he didn't need to find one when footfalls sounded behind him and then Bradley spoke up.

"If ever there was a man I didn't want to meet again, it'd be you," he said, standing at Rattigan's shoulder.

Victor rolled his shoulders, seemingly ready to repay Bradley for the incident in the railroad office, but to Rattigan's surprise, Bradley backed down first. He placed a calm hand on Rattigan's shoulder and ushered him away. As Victor sneered with contempt, he and Bradley retreated with as much dignity as they could muster.

"I'm obliged for your help," Rattigan said when they were heading back into town.

"I only came to show Victor he doesn't

scare me, but I'm not surprised you wanted to run away," Bradley said with a scowl.

"I thought we both agreed that going back to Silver Creek wouldn't be healthy."

"It won't, except I'm not running away with my tail between my legs." Bradley smiled thinly. "But luckily this morning I got me some new partners. They won't make mistakes like you did."

Rattigan resisted the urge to retort and joined Bradley in moving on to the law office. On the wall outside, a new Wanted poster told him the basic details that a bounty had been posted on Corbin Metz's head of $2,000, along with the fact that he was wanted either dead or alive.

"You've decided to become a bounty hunter?" Rattigan asked, unable to mask the surprise in his tone.

"Sure." With a smile on his lips Bradley gestured at the door and a few moments later two men came out. They both held a copy of the poster. "We three are heading to the Sagebrush saloon to plan our first move."

Rattigan was too surprised to do anything other than join them. One bounty hunter seemed to be angry about something and he walked several steps behind them. The second man was young and nervous.

He scurried along beside them like an eager hound before scampering on ahead to reach the saloon and then the bar first. When they all had full glasses of whiskey before them, the young man identified himself as a newcomer to town, Percy Jedson. The angry-looking man wouldn't provide a name and he edged away for a few paces, although he stayed close enough to hear what they discussed.

"So you men are going to work together to find Corbin, are you?" Rattigan asked.

"Bradley and me are," Percy said. He nodded at the silent man. "We're not sure about him yet."

The angry-looking man was avoiding Rattigan's eye, so he turned to Bradley's fresh-faced associate. He resisted the urge to make an obvious taunt about a young man who didn't look old enough to be drinking whiskey never mind tracking down a dangerous gunslinger.

"Why do you reckon you can find him?"

"I don't. I just reckon that a share of the bounty will be better than cleaning out the stables." Percy raised the whiskey glass to his lips. His first sip made his eyes water and he coughed twice before continuing. "When we drag Corbin into town, so much lead will be weighing him down, you won't be strong enough to move him."

Rattigan blew out his cheeks in bemusement. "Is this your first bounty hunt, kid?"

"Yeah." Percy slammed his glass down on the bar and squared up to him. "What does that matter?"

"I just hope it won't be your last."

Percy's face darkened, but before he could retort, Bradley stepped between them.

"I may have saved my new friend from being a stable boy," he said, "but he's already had more good ideas than you'll ever have. He wouldn't be so stupid as to give a gunslinger a ride into town and then let him steal our silver."

"We both made that mistake," Rattigan said with a weary air that acknowledged a pointless argument was now inevitable.

"I said we should leave Corbin afoot. If you'd done that, I'd still have a job and Frank would still have gotten paid."

"And you wouldn't have to get yourself killed on a damn fool mission to claim a bounty on a notorious gunslinger."

"At least I've got the guts to do something about our problems instead of trying to run away like a scared kid."

Rattigan leaned forward. "Except I'm staying now, so maybe I'll claim that bounty for myself."

Bradley smirked as the argument took a direction that Rattigan hadn't anticipated, but having made his boast, he didn't feel like retracting it and losing face. While Bradley sipped his whiskey and then licked his lips in apparent triumph at having forced Rattigan to make his claim, the other member of the group broke his silence with an oath. Then he shoved his glass away, sending whiskey spraying across the bar before the glass slid over the edge and smashed on the floor.

"I knew bounty hunters were scum," he said. "Seeing it doesn't make this any easier."

Percy and Bradley turned around to stand beside Rattigan, their former disagreement forgotten about.

"Then you should have looked in a mirror before you went in the law office." Bradley said. "Then you'd have learned that lesson quicker."

"I wouldn't, because I'm no bounty hunter. I'm Delano Metz, Corbin's brother."

Bradley winced and then gave a slow nod. "Corbin claimed he was coming to town to see you."

"Corbin claimed a lot of things," Delano said with a snarl. "The last time I saw him, he claimed he hadn't shot up Marshal Dagwood, and I believe him. I intend to prove he's innocent, and men like you don't make that any easier."

"So what's your plan to find him?" Rattigan asked.

"The simplest one, which means I'm not joining you." Delano walked along the line of men. "Don't get in my way."

Then Delano headed to the door, which he shoved aside so strongly the batwings creaked back and forth several times before stilling.

"That solves one mystery," Percy said. "Do you reckon we should follow him?"

"Sure," Bradley said with a smile. "After he followed us, it's only fair."

"He knows nothing," Rattigan said. He slipped between them to lean on the bar. "Neither do you two."

"Maybe we don't, but I don't believe you've got the guts to go through with your boast," Bradley said.

"I'm no bounty hunter." Rattigan pondered, but despite his small chance of success, the thought of acting positively enthused him. "That doesn't mean I can't try to save our jobs and the mine by finding the stolen silver."

"How?"

Rattigan shrugged. "I don't know yet, but I

do know I'm not riding around in the hope I'll stumble across a clue that leads me to Corbin. So I'll see what I can learn here."

Bradley sneered, proving he'd correctly summed up his and Percy's plan.

"You'll fail." Bradley tapped his chest and then Percy's. "The next time you see us, your brother will have the bounty on Corbin."

Rattigan downed his whiskey. "If you ride off after Corbin, the next time I see you, my brother will be dead."

FOUR

"I'm sure now that Corbin's not at the house," Percy Jedson said, raising his head above the boulder.

Bradley sighed. The scene hadn't changed in the three hours since they'd slipped into hiding.

"How can you be sure?"

Percy smiled. "Because my young eyes are sharper than your old eyes and when Delano just went to the barn, he walked real slow. That means he's not worried."

"For a kid on his first bounty hunt, you're sure of yourself." Bradley pointed at several riders that were coming down Dead Man's Canyon. "Although you might not be the only one."

They stayed behind their covering line of

small boulders and, when the men came closer, Bradley confirmed the lead rider was Victor Greystone.

"I thought I'd warned your brother that you're not to leave town," Victor said when he'd drawn up in front of them.

The other six riders spread out cutting off their escape routes to either side, so Bradley didn't wait to find out what their intentions were. From behind the low boulder, he raised his drawn gun. The sight made Victor narrow his eyes while his men turned to him for guidance.

"We aim to claim the bounty that's been posted on Corbin's head," Bradley said using a light conversational tone.

Victor snorted a laugh. "You won't find him standing around here watching his brother's house. Corbin's long gone."

Bradley shrugged. "Men who were too yellow to take on Corbin back in Bear Rock can't tell me what to do."

The railroad men tensed making Percy edge his hand toward his gun, but Victor gave a gesture ordering them to back away.

"No man has ever drawn a gun on me twice either," he said with a thin smile before he peeled away.

In a line the riders followed Victor. Each man stayed for long enough to sneer at Bradley and Percy before they trooped off around the boulders. They paraded down to the house, their arrival encouraging Delano to come out of the barn, but Victor didn't stop.

At a slow pace and in single file the men rode between the house and the barn before they sped up to a gallop as they headed to the entrance to the canyon. Even from some distance, Bradley gathered that Delano was bemused as he set his hands on his hips.

"So Victor wants Delano to know he's searched in the canyon," Bradley said as Delano headed to his house. "He hopes that'll make him do something stupid such as trying to warn Corbin."

"Which has ruined everything for us," Percy grumbled.

"You've still got a lot to learn, kid." Bradley winked. "Now it's time to teach you something."

Bradley holstered his gun and set off walking purposefully around the boulders. Percy trailed along behind. When they reached clear ground, his young associate joined him and he bounded along sideways while waving his arms as he struggled to articulate how bad an idea this endeavor was.

"Walking up to the house and letting Delano know we're watching him will make things even worse. After that, he'll never let his brother get within five miles of here."

"Perhaps you should have paired up with my brother." Bradley stopped beside the barn and turned to Percy. "That's the sort of nonsense he'd say."

With that, Bradley walked on. Wisely, when Percy joined him he kept quiet. They were halfway between the barn and the house when Delano came out of the house with a rifle in hand.

"I told you back in the Sagebrush saloon not to get in my way," he said.

"That's not neighborly," Bradley said with

a smile. "We just want to make sure your no-account brother gets strung up."

Delano walked up to Bradley with his rifle held across his chest. When Bradley stood his ground, Delano frowned and turned to Percy, who backed up Bradley's truculent posture by squaring up to him, but Delano's movement had been only a distraction.

With a quick motion, Delano jerked up the rifle butt aiming to slap Bradley about the side of the head. At the last moment Bradley turned away, but the wood still clipped the point of his chin and knocked him aside. With an angry grunt Percy moved in, but he stomped to a halt when Delano snapped the rifle around to aim it at his stomach.

"Back away or I'll blast you in two," Delano said.

Percy stood tall, his fingers inching toward his holster as he clearly weighed up his chances.

"Do as he says," Bradley said from the ground. "My brother was right about him. He knows nothing."

"I was right, too," Delano said. "All bounty

hunters are scum."

Percy's eyes flared, an angry retort seeming to be on his lips, but then sense defeated his growing rage and he backed away. Bradley took his time in getting to his feet, exaggerating his hurt, and then moved to follow him.

That encouraged Delano to lower his rifle so Bradley rocked his weight back on to his toes. He leaped forward while aiming a scything punch at Delano's face. Delano tried to jerk away from the blow, but he wasn't quick enough to avoid Bradley's fist crunching into his cheek, bending him double.

Bradley followed through by grabbing Delano's rifle and hurling it away. Then he was on him. A rapid flurry of blows knocked Delano from side to side until he delivered a short-armed uppercut to his jaw. For a moment Delano stood with his back arched before he toppled over to land on his back with a thud, raising a cloud of dust.

Bradley stood over him. "If you ever hit me again, I'll kill you."

Delano fingered his jaw. "If you ever come back to Dead Man's Canyon, I'll kill you."

"I'm glad we understand each other."

Bradley tipped his hat with mock pleasantness. Then, before Delano could retort, he turned on his heel and joined Percy.

"So what did we gain from that escapade?" Percy said when they were heading back to the boulders.

Bradley didn't reply until they'd wended their way through the boulders and unhobbled their horses. He poked at his tender chin and then pointed at the barn.

"While you were confronting Delano, I looked in the barn. It was empty, but it seems he was walking slowly so that he could scuff his feet and cover up wheel tracks, but he didn't mask them all, so I reckon a wagon was in there recently."

Percy noted Bradley's grin and then smiled. "Yours?"

"That's my guess." Bradley examined the ground. "So we need to find out where it went."

With that, they headed back down the

canyon. They rode slowly and took a snaking path, and they were rewarded when, on a patch of soft ground at the entrance to the canyon, they passed deep wheel ruts that headed toward Delano's house. When they came to harder ground where the ruts were no longer visible, Bradley drew his horse to a halt and noted the direction the ruts had been taking going away from the house.

"What's over there?" Percy asked when he noticed where he was looking.

"There's nothing for a half day's ride. Then there's the ghost town of Red Creek." Bradley smiled. "Apparently, Corbin once lived there."

"Sometimes the last place you'd expect someone to be is where they are."

"You speak a lot of sense," Bradley said. "I reckon I'll enjoy riding with a new partner."

Percy grinned widely as they rode off. "So what will your old partner be doing now?"

Bradley snorted. "My brother won't have done nothing useful yet. He'll still be in the Sagebrush saloon, moistening throats and asking questions."

Percy sighed as he noted the baked-dry terrain that stretched away into the distance.

"Perhaps I should have joined him instead," he said with a laugh. "I like the sound of spending a quiet afternoon in the saloon."

* * *

Rattigan ducked under Thornton Packer's first aimed blow and then side-stepped away from his second wild punch, but he couldn't avoid the thrown chair. It smashed into the back of his right shoulder, knocking him forward against the bar.

Unfortunately, the bartender was defending the bar and taking on anyone who got too close. An empty whiskey bottle came crashing down toward his head forcing Rattigan to flinch sideways.

The bottle whistled through the air so close to his face he felt the breeze on his cheek before it smashed down on the bar. With the bartender being unbalanced,

Rattigan took the opportunity to inflict some damage of his own and he grabbed the man's jacket and hoisted him forward.

The bartender's chest slapped down on the bar and then, with all the spilled liquor and broken glass beneath him, he went sliding on until he tumbled headfirst on to the floor. Luckily, the bartender's flailing limbs knocked over Thornton so with space opening up, Rattigan leaned back against the bar and took stock of the situation.

Several fights were on-going. Most were one on one, some were several on one, and one fight in the middle of the Sagebrush's saloon room was one against many. About thirty men were slugging it out and, as far as Rattigan could tell, half of them were railroad workers who had rolled into town eager to spend this week's wages.

The other half was just townsfolk in a bad mood. As Rattigan had started the trouble when he'd asked too many questions about Victor's and Corbin's past, he searched for the safest route away.

The brawl had become localized around

him with those who had been on the periphery when the fight had started congregating by the door. He doubted he could reach the door unscathed and, when Thornton started clawing his way to his feet by grasping his leg and tugging, he shook him off and went in the opposite direction.

He rolled over the bar and dropped down on the other side where he found he wasn't alone. Warner Earhart, one of the men he'd been questioning when the fight had broken out, was kneeling bent over on the floor with his hands covering his head.

Warner was an old friend of Marshal Dagwood. He'd been eager to talk, but when he registered that Rattigan had joined him, his deep frown said he now regretted accepting his offer of a drink.

"I told you that asking questions about railroad men in a railroad town was a bad idea," Warner said.

Rattigan was about to agree with him when a bottle smashed into the wall above his head forcing him to adopt Warner's pose. Doubled-over, he let the glass shards shower down on his back and they were soon followed by a row of glasses, a chair and then a thrown man.

As that man groaned and struggled to rise, Rattigan decided this hiding-place wasn't as safe as he'd hoped it'd be so he crawled toward the corner of the bar. He'd yet to reach it when a gunshot blasted, the sound cutting through the hubbub and creating sudden silence.

"Stop fighting now or I'll throw you all in a cell," Marshal Eddie Bishop demanded from the door.

For several seconds silence reigned, but the hope of a quick end to the skirmish died out when a window smashed and loud recriminations started up.

"It's time to get out of here," Warner said at Rattigan's side before crawling on.

Warner appeared to know where he was going so Rattigan followed. Sure enough, Warner crawled through a door behind the bar where he waited for Rattigan to join him. Then they gained their feet and scurried away through two more doors to reach a back exit. Only then did they pause for breath and listen to the sounds of chaos emanating from the saloon.

"We need to be elsewhere when the marshal pieces together how that fight got started," Rattigan said.

"I reckon the only thing he'll care about is that it finishes." Warner winced when another window smashed. "Although it wouldn't hurt to be on the other side of town right now."

Rattigan nodded and adopting a casual gait they made their way back to the main drag. They slowed as they passed the saloon where the marshal and Deputy Crane were dragging people outside before they moved on toward the station.

"For the sake of my future well-being, what *exactly* did I say that got those men so angry?" Rattigan said.

"You asked the railroad man Thornton Packer why everyone was sure Corbin killed the marshal when Victor was the only witness." Warner shrugged when Rattigan raised a quizzical eyebrow. "Men who work for the railroad don't like what that implies."

"You didn't get angry."

"Corbin is a ruthless man." Warner frowned. "So is Victor."

Rattigan turned to the office. Two days ago, on this spot, he'd seen Victor standing at the office window, and he now knew that Marshal Dagwood had been found lying dead outside that window.

"So I need to ask someone who knows the truth."

Warner smiled and stopped. The saloon was now quiet.

"You don't want to meet Corbin again and Victor won't answer. Either way, Victor left town earlier."

"Then I'd better ask my questions before Victor returns," Rattigan said with a smile.

FIVE

Bradley and Percy only survived Corbin Metz's first ferocious volley of gunshots by diving on to their chests and hugging the dirt. Then Corbin ran with his head down toward the derelict saloon, but by the time Bradley could take aim at him, Corbin had gone to ground.

Both men leaped to their feet and hurried into hiding behind the wagon Corbin had stolen. Bradley checked in the back. An empty space confronted him, so he turned to the saloon. They had found wheel ruts at regular intervals, but they hadn't been sure they were following Corbin until they'd ridden into this gunfight.

"There's nowhere left to run, Corbin," Bradley shouted. "Either walk out of the saloon or come out feet first, it doesn't matter none to us."

"If you want me, you'll have to come in and get me," Corbin shouted from inside the doorway.

Bradley caught Percy's eye and winked, showing he'd been goading Corbin into confirming where in the building he was hiding. Then, with hand gestures alone, he told Percy to head around to the back of the saloon while he moved closer to the door.

Percy scurried off with his head down and gained the side of the saloon in moments. Bradley waited until Percy reached the back corner of the building before he hurried on to stand beside the front corner.

The building's roof had collapsed down on to the ceiling of the saloon room leaving the walls bowed and debris lying on the ground. With his gun thrust to the side, Bradley picked his way over that debris while keeping his back to the wall and he reached the only window on the front of the building without mishap.

The area before the door was visible

through the window, but not Corbin. So he doubled over and shuffled along with his head below the window to the doorway. For his last pace he stepped over a heap of wood and his heel caught a plank, making it roll and thud to the ground.

The noise was loud enough to be heard inside and worse, that started an avalanche of rolling wood that cascaded across the doorway. With all chance lost of sneaking up on the door unnoticed, Bradley sprinted inside while keeping low.

Then, with his back to the wall, he swung around. Corbin wasn't visible. The back door through which Percy planned to enter was straight ahead. Only three obstacles constricted his vision and behind which Corbin could have hidden.

In the center of the room was a large post that held up the ceiling, to his left were six barrels beneath a plank that had served as the bar and to his right was the collapsed staircase. Bradley jerked from side to side confirming Corbin wasn't hiding behind the post while the wreckage of the staircase was too insubstantial to cover his quarry.

So, with his gun trained on the barrels, he waited for Percy to reach the back door, which he did after a minute. With nods and gestures Bradley reported on the situation silently, so Percy slipped inside and faced the bar.

Then Bradley walked stealthily toward the nearest barrel. The area beyond the bar became visible, but there were no shadows and he decided that Corbin wasn't hiding there.

"Could he have escaped through the back door?" Bradley asked.

"I reached the door too quickly for him to get out," Percy said. "Even if he had, the ground at the back is flat and I saw nobody out there."

Percy took three purposeful steps toward the barrels. The plank on the top was heavy and it appeared to be lying firmly in place, but the two men agreed the only place Corbin could be hiding was inside the barrels.

Percy aimed at the barrel at his end and

Bradley took the one closest to him. In a coordinated move they fired three times, planting a single bullet in each barrel. Then Bradley carried on to hole the barrels Percy had already shot at while Percy held his fire.

As Bradley reloaded, Percy fired at Bradley's barrels. Corbin couldn't have avoided their assault unscathed, but they had to reclaim his body so as Percy reloaded, Bradley approached the bar while trying to work out how they'd dislodge the plank of wood.

A gunshot blasted. Bradley turned around and confirmed that Percy hadn't fired, but sadly his young partner was dropping to his knees, his gun falling from his grasp. Then he keeled over on to his chest while clutching his back, but before he hit the floor, Bradley ran for the bar.

Something moved beyond Percy's body so he leaped forward. He hit the floor with his chest and slid along until he came to a halt behind the first barrel after which he drew up his legs and rolled into hiding.

Only then did he try to work out where the

movement had been. When he decided it had come from an unexpected direction, he got up on to his haunches and slapped his gun hand on the bar.

Without looking he sighted the approximate area of the hole in the ceiling that had been made when the staircase had fallen away. He fired once before he raised his head. Then he blasted lead around the edges of the hole, hoping he'd get lucky and the fragile ceiling wouldn't block every shot.

After five shots he stopped firing and ducked to reload. He was slamming in the final bullet when scrambling sounded and then a clatter. When he bobbed back up, he faced the situation he'd expected.

Corbin had dropped down through the hole, but he'd landed awkwardly amid the debris below and he'd tipped over on to his side. Bradley tore off a quick shot that kicked splinters from the wood inches away from Corbin's right arm.

He didn't get to fire a second time when Corbin snapped up his arm and returned fire. His gunshot from a difficult position sliced into the wood beside Bradley's left hand making him jerk his hand away while ducking.

A second shot hammered into the barrel and the old wood wasn't strong enough to withstand the slug. It tore out through the other side and cut through the edge of Bradley's sleeve, so Bradley scurried away.

Doubled over he ran behind the barrels, reaching the endmost one without Corbin firing again. When he turned around, Corbin was no longer visible, but Bradley was now wise to Corbin's tactics.

A flurry of dust rising from the floor told him that Corbin had run across the saloon room and slipped behind the post. So confidently Bradley stood up and leveled his gun on the post ensuring that, no matter which way Corbin moved, he'd receive a bellyful of lead.

"Have you got more fight in you than your new partner had?" Corbin said.

"I have enough to take you," Bradley said, moving out from behind the bar.

"Then you'd better take me alive." Corbin

snorted a laugh. "Or you'll never find out what I did with the silver."

"I'm here for the bounty only. I'll get that whether you're alive or dead."

Bradley moved sideways quietly to gain a different angle on the post and to ensure he'd moved away from the position he had been in when he'd spoken. His caution paid off, as he'd taken only two paces when Corbin slipped his gun into view.

Corbin fired blind, although his shot still whistled past Bradley's left arm as he picked out his current position accurately. Bradley resisted the urge to return fire and so tell Corbin where he was, but Corbin surprised him when he came out fast and on his haunches.

Bradley jerked his gun down, but he had yet to shoot at Corbin's unexpected position when Corbin fired. Pain lanced down his right arm. His gun clattered to the floor as he grasped his bloodied arm.

Bradley shook his head to clear his senses. Then he moved for the gun with his left hand, but Corbin fired again and sent the weapon skittering away across the saloon floor. Bradley staggered toward it, but the movement made the pain in his arm spread to his neck and shoulders. So he shuffled around to face Corbin, finding he had now trained his gun on his chest.

"There'll be no bounty for you today," Corbin said. Then he fired.

This time Bradley only heard the gunshot. He must have blacked out as the next he knew he was lying on his back facing the dirty and bowed saloon ceiling. His body felt numb and he judged that was probably a good thing as it distanced him from whatever damage Corbin had inflicted.

His small hope that Corbin might not bother to finish him off fled when Corbin loomed over him. He aimed his gun at Bradley's head and raised an eyebrow with a silent question.

"Go to hell," Bradley said, his voice croaking in his dry mouth.

"As you wish," Corbin said with a shrug.

Bradley let his head loll to the side. Five feet away lay Percy and to Bradley's surprise, his eyes were open and moving. Bradley blinked and forced his eyes to refocus on his young partner.

He hadn't been mistaken; Percy was still alive. Better still, he'd reclaimed the gun he'd dropped when he'd been shot.

"Wait," Bradley spluttered, but Corbin didn't appear surprised at his apparent change of heart. "What do you want to know?"

"How did Victor react when he read the coffin's inscription?"

"He didn't have time to read it." Bradley then spoke quickly as Corbin narrowed his eyes, this answer clearly not being the one he had wanted to hear. "When he heard that the initials KD were on it, he was mighty angry."

Corbin nodded with approval. "I'll settle for that reaction."

Bradley licked his lips as he searched for something else to say that would keep Corbin's interest until Percy could act.

"Why do you hate Victor?" he asked.

"He killed Marshal Ken Dagwood and

convinced everyone I'd done it." Corbin rubbed his jaw as he thought back. "I didn't think anyone but my brother would believe my story, so I fled. Now I'm back to make him suffer."

"I believe you." Bradley forced a defiant smile. "That won't stop me claiming the bounty on your head."

"Which is as it should be."

Corbin laughed loudly. Then his gun hand tensed. A gunshot cracked, the sound echoing in the room and making Bradley flinch. Then, to his relief, Corbin twitched and tipped over to land with a clatter beside him.

Behind his fallen body, Percy was lying on his back with his gun resting on his chest, the effort required to shoot seeming to have exhausted his failing strength. Bradley rolled his shoulders, but before he could act, Corbin levered himself up to a kneeling position.

He felt the back of his head and, when he examined the fingers, they were bloody. Then he gained his feet, but he stumbled and stomped forward with uncertain steps. Corbin took faltering steps toward the door.

He managed five paces. Then his left leg gave way and he went scooting to the side until he slammed shoulder first into the post. A heavy crack sounded as Corbin slid down the post to sit on the floor.

Percy didn't appear able to fight back again, which made Corbin turn up the corners of his mouth with a grim smile. Then he raised his gun arm to aim at him. Corbin struggled to keep his hand steady, so Bradley searched for his own gun, finding it lying four feet away, and then rolled on to his side, but the effort sent pain coursing through his side making him roll up into a ball.

When the pain receded, a gunshot blasted and Percy twitched before he breathed out a sighing gasp. He didn't draw breath again. Thankfully Corbin hadn't aimed at Bradley yet. His eyes were glassy and the length of post where he'd rested his head was red and wet.

Bradley shuffled across the floor like a

sidewinder until he could slap his left hand on his gun. He swung it around to aim at Corbin, who regarded him with half-closed eyes. Then his head lowered until his chin rested on his chest.

He exhaled a long, rattling breath and his gun fell from his grasp as he tipped over on to his side. For long moments he didn't breathe in again. Then another loud crack broke the silence.

This time the noise continued as the floor shook and dirt rained down on Bradley's head, blanketing him in a layer of white dust. Then Bradley was confronted by the strange sight of the ceiling getting closer.

Several moments passed before he realized what had happened, but by then it was too late to act. He closed his eyes a moment before the saloon collapsed in on him.

SIX

Rattigan backhanded the door open. Earlier, Victor had returned to town, but he hadn't come here so the second floor railroad office was in darkness. He side-stepped inside and closed the door behind him.

This time, every inch of movement made the door creak, the sound unnaturally loud in the otherwise quiet room. By the time the door was shut, Rattigan's heart was hammering and his harsh breathing was so loud he felt sure someone would hear it and then come to investigate.

But he had to find something that made the risk he was taking worthwhile so he moved stealthily to the large desk that dominated the office. He rattled the drawers. All of them opened except for the bottom one on the left, so he concentrated on this one.

Using a letter-opening knife he found on the desk, he poked around in a gap on the underside of the desk. A few prods provided a satisfying click after which the drawer edged open, but he found only money.

Disappointed, he wriggled the drawer in the hope it'd lock itself. It didn't, so he examined the other drawers. Most were empty and the others contained ledgers filled with pages of figures and neat writing.

Using the moonlight from the window, the little he could read detailed routine railroad business. Rattigan sighed and examined the cabinets along the wall. Unfortunately, these contained only liquor.

So he searched for something he'd missed on his first examination that might shed light on Victor's activities and lead him to Corbin. All he found of interest was a door on the opposite wall, so he explored the small room beyond.

It was empty, but the moonlight shining in through the gap between the shutters hit the wall at an acute angle and highlighted a square that was raised from the surrounding wall. He tapped the center, hearing a hollow sound, so he got to work.

Within moments he'd located the catch that made a hidden door spring open and reveal a safe. So Rattigan flexed his fingers and put them to the combination lock. He had never tried to open a safe before, but with his ear pressed to the cold metal, he had turned the dial for only a fraction when the door thudded against his cheek making him flinch away.

"Either I have a skill I never knew I had or. . . ." Rattigan trailed off as the alternative hit him.

He hadn't expected he'd be able to break into the office quietly, and yet he'd found an open door. He'd broken into the desk without difficulty and now he'd found a hidden safe unlocked.

With the feeling that something was wrong growing, he rummaged around inside the safe, but he felt nothing. In irritation, he closed the safe door using more force than he'd intended to, and the door made a metallic clunk that echoed in the small room.

Even the shutters creaked and one shutter swung open. So while thinking through what he should do next, he turned to the window and then gasped. A face was on the other side of the revealed window.

Rattigan backed away for a pace and, when he got over his surprise, he recognized the man as being Delano Metz. He was kneeling on a ledge outside.

"What are you doing here?" Delano asked.

"The same as you, although I'd guess you got here first," Rattigan said.

Delano nodded. "I reckon I might have found proof that Victor killed the marshal."

"Which is?"

Delano frowned, seeming as if he wouldn't answer before he shrugged.

"You seem different to the others, so I guess it'll do no harm. Marshal Dagwood and the railroad didn't argue about security, but about the bribes Dagwood wouldn't take to look the other way." Delano patted his pocket. "But Victor bribed others and now I might be able to prove that."

"You might, but from the way your brother shot up the town when he rode off with our silver, you might prove he's guilty, after all."

Delano frowned. "I know. If I get the chance, I'll get your silver back, and if I'm wrong about Corbin, I'll deliver justice myself. I'm not letting no. . . ."

Delano looked as if he'd say more, but he cocked an ear and a moment later a distant warning cry went up. Rattigan hurried to the door. Quick footfalls were coming up the main stairs. He turned back to the window, but Delano had gone.

Then down below a thud sounded and a few moments later wheels creaked. Rattigan searched for an escape route, but the footfalls were coming down the corridor outside. So he closed the office door and the hidden door before he hurried to the window.

The tail end of Delano's wagon was disappearing from view as the door outside crashed open and what sounded like, from the footfalls, three men spilled inside. He was on the upper floor at the side of the building and he judged that the drop was too great to attempt when he didn't have something below to break his fall.

The ledge that Delano had stood on ran along the wall beside the window. It was only a foot wide, but he clambered up on to the sill and edged out on to the ledge. Inside, the newcomers hurried across the main office and they wasted no time before bursting into the smaller room giving Rattigan no time to close the shutters. So he pressed himself to the wall and tried to avoid moving.

"I told you someone was up here," Victor's unmistakable barking voice proclaimed. "The shutters are open, and the safe's been broken into."

"Is anything missing?" Marshal Bishop said as he headed to the window.

"Everything! It's all gone. Every note, letter and document about our procedures has been stolen."

Rattigan sensed that Bishop stuck his head outside, but he didn't dare check in case the movement alerted him. Then Victor's anger made the marshal step back and slam the shutters closed.

"Whoever stole them must reckon they contain something interesting, but he won't have gone far. I'll post Deputy Crane outside to make sure he doesn't come back."

Purposeful footfalls sounded heading back across the room as Bishop collected Crane and left. Rattigan sensed that Victor dallied in the office so he didn't try the shutters, but with the possibility of immediate discovery now passed, he thought about his predicament.

This proved to be a bad idea. The darkness below drew him forward. He stood tall and pressed himself to the wall, but he still felt as if he was leaning forward. With his heart hammering he spread his arms and flattened his hands to the wall.

This didn't help as now it felt as if the wall itself was tilting over. He tried to move his feet to seek a better footing, but his legs felt as if they were too heavy to move and he stayed where he was.

He exerted greater force and this time he jerked his right leg forward by a foot and his boot landed on air. With the wall seeming to press against his back, he toppled. He twisted and tried to regain his former perch, but he fell, suffering a gut-wrenching moment when he was airborne until his flailing hands slapped against the ledge.

He hung on with his body at full stretch and pressed to the wall beneath the ledge. He felt sure that Victor in the office should have heard him, but a minute passed without any noises coming from up above. Then Bishop and Crane approached while engaging in a quiet conversation that, when they passed below him, he was able to discern.

"This robbery is a strange one," Deputy Crane said.

"If Victor's concerned about it, so are we," Marshal Bishop said. "We follow up his story no matter what our personal feelings."

"Sure." Crane chuckled. "But I can't help wondering if you're leaving me here to guard the building or Victor."

Bishop lowered his voice and Rattigan couldn't hear his reply, but his comment made both men laugh. Then footfalls sounded as Victor left the building, which stopped the laughter and made the lawmen walk away.

Silence followed for a minute so Rattigan craned his neck. The lawmen were heading out of view, but Victor wasn't visible. He presumed he was below him. He turned back to the wall.

The motion made cramps shoot down his right arm reminding that he couldn't dangle here for much longer, so he edged his right hand toward the window. A splinter jabbed into his index finger making an oath slip from his lips and worse, he flinched his hand away.

His left hand couldn't take the strain and then he was falling, this time with no way to stop himself. He fell for only a moment before he slammed down on the ground in a confusion of arms of legs that, when he tried to get to his feet, he found weren't all his.

Groggily he extricated himself from

Victor, who had broken his fall. Unfortunately, Victor got his wits about him quickly and he drew his gun on him.

"You have some explaining to do," Victor said.

With Rattigan still feeling shaky after his fall, he didn't respond so Victor bounded in and crashed the gun against the side of his head sending him reeling. Rattigan stumbled away for two paces.

Then, when the main drag appeared to sway, he dropped to his knees. He blinked rapidly, but that failed to stop his vision moving. Then, from behind, he heard Victor advancing on him.

Even that concern couldn't make him gather his strength. He toppled forward to lie face down in the dirt groaning. Cold metal jabbed into the back of his neck.

"Get off me," Rattigan said, his voice muffled.

"I've had enough of you and your brother," Victor said in his ear. "Give me back what you stole and I'll make this quick."

Rattigan figured that Victor wouldn't

shoot while he thought he had the stolen documents so he struggled. Victor subdued him easily by pressing a knee down on his back, but that bought Rattigan enough time when Marshal Bishop spoke up from nearby.

"What's happening there?" he demanded, his rapid footfalls closing on them.

The pressure on Rattigan's back lessened.

"I caught the man who broke into my office," Victor called. Then he leaned over Rattigan and lowered his voice. "The marshal will throw you in the jailhouse for this, but don't go thinking I can't get to you in there. You'll never leave your cell alive."

* * *

"Is he dead?" a voice asked in the dark.

"No. He's still with us. Perhaps we can help him."

A skeptical snort sounded. "You can try if you want to, but I'm not wasting my time. Look at him. He'll never survive until you can get him to help."

Bradley decided this conversation was too worrying to dwell on and he let his mind wander. A timeless period of darkness followed until he enjoyed a comforting dream in which he was riding along an endless prairie with the wind making the grass to either side undulate like a green ocean.

This was the landscape of his childhood and he knew it was a dream, but he managed to stay asleep. Sadly, an impenetrable darkness soon spread across the dream prairie. A more worrying dream engulfed him in which he huddled in a small space and a disembodied voice called out to him for help.

When he recognized the voice as being Corbin's, he fought to open his eyes. With a wrenching feeling, the dream broke apart to reveal light. He found himself lying awake on a bed in a room with stone walls and a single moonlit window.

The men who had spoken earlier weren't here and neither was anyone else. He tried to raise himself, but the effort failed to move him and he stayed on his back. So he blinked rapidly to banish the dream that still felt as if it might return and tried to recall what had happened.

He remembered Corbin shooting him. He remembered Percy and Corbin shooting each other. Then both men had died before the saloon roof collapsed in on him, but after that he could recall only people talking and then dreams.

As the most vivid of these dreams had involved moving, he presumed that someone had found him and they had taken him to help. He called out, but he made no sound so he tried again without effect.

After three more attempts, he heard his own voice emerging as a croaking whisper. As the effort had exhausted him and darkness was narrowing his vision, he gave up trying to attract attention.

Instead he concentrated on breathing and being patient. He must have dozed again, this time dreamlessly, as the next he knew a woman was standing over him. She was of indeterminate age, dressed in a nun's habit and sporting an aggrieved expression, as if he'd somehow done something wrong while he'd been asleep. Bradley was more inter-ested in the bowl of water she was holding.

"I'm Sister Mary," she declared as she brought the bowl to Bradley's lips and helped him take a long sip. "You're now in good hands."

"I sure am pleased to see you," Bradley said, or at least he tried to say that. What emerged was a series of hoarse grunts.

Mary helped him to drink another sip and this time the moisture wetted his throat and let him speak clearly, but Mary stopped him before he finished his statement.

"Don't waste your energy by talking. Rest."

"I've done all the resting I mean to do." Bradley flexed his back and tried to rise. He managed to move for only a few inches before he accepted he was too weak to sit up and he flopped back down. "I guess if you want me to stay here, we could do a deal."

"I make deals with no man, but I'm here to serve."

"Then get a message to Marshal Bishop.

Tell him that Corbin Metz is dead and that Bradley Cooke is here and I want my bounty."

"Our mission hospital is only a few miles from Bear Rock so I could speak to Marshal Bishop, but not about matters of killing and—" Mary broke off when Bradley made a lunge at her.

Strangely, his right hand didn't move and take hold of her habit as he'd intended, but his expression was angry enough to make her sigh with concern.

Bradley lowered his voice. "I'll give you fifty dollars to take that message to him."

"I'm not interested in money. As Saint Paul told us, we're all children of God and so—"

"You're children of God, eh? In that case it'll probably cost me one hundred dollars."

Mary had gritted her teeth before he'd finished speaking, as if his interruptions had annoyed her more than his words. She leaned over him and fussed with his blanket.

"Put aside your thoughts of dollars and death."

Bradley flexed his back against the bed. Then he made a determined lunge for Mary's habit, aiming to drag her down to his eye level and impress upon her the urgency of his need to get a message to the marshal.

Again his hand didn't move, so he lowered his gaze to his sleeve. He gulped. He no longer had a right arm.

SEVEN

"I hope Victor will be fine," Rattigan said, facing Marshal Bishop through the bars. "It was an accident."

"That makes you the most accident-prone man I've ever met," Bishop said. "You accidentally brought a gunslinger back to town. Then you accidentally started a fight in the Sagebrush saloon. Now you've accidentally accosted the railroad boss."

When Rattigan's cellmate, the burly Thornton Packer, grunted with irritation, Rattigan decided the best way to deal with the accusation was lightly, as the story Victor must have told Bishop would have been at odds with what had actually happened. He shrugged and lowered his tone to a concerned one.

"I was heading to the station, but I wasn't looking where I was going and I bumped into Victor." He rubbed a bruise on his elbow and gave a hopeful smile. "I reckon I hurt myself as much as I hurt him."

"You're right about that. When I found Victor helping you to your feet, he was so groggy it looked like you'd dropped on him from a great height."

Rattigan couldn't think of an appropriate response so Bishop headed away from the cells. When the door between the jailhouse and the law office closed, Rattigan lay on his cot. Worryingly, Warner Earhart was in the next cell, and he clambered on to the cot that stood nearest to him and spoke quietly.

"I doubt Bishop will accept your excuses. He pulled me in for being one of the ringleaders behind the saloon brawl." He gestured at the other cells and at Thornton, who was lying on his cot with his back turned, although he was so still he was clearly listening to him. "Most of these men are from that fight."

As Rattigan remembered Thornton from

the fight, he resolved to avoid catching his eye. He lay on his back and tried to will himself to sleep. With the many unresolved questions of the last few days, this proved to be hard and it was long into the night before he dozed, and even then he awoke to every sound in the jailhouse.

So he was already alert when at first light a creak sounded nearby, although he was surprised when two hands slapped down on his collar and hoisted him off his cot. He had just registered that his cellmate had accosted him when Thornton pressed him up against the bars.

"I've got a message from Victor," Thornton said. "He says you stole something from him."

Rattigan slapped his hands to Thornton's wrists and tugged, but he couldn't dislodge him and that only encouraged Thornton to gather a tighter grip and shove him up the bars until he was on tiptoes.

"I've got a message for Victor," Rattigan said. "If you harm me, he won't get it back."

"That's the wrong answer." Thornton

straightened his arms, thrusting Rattigan off the floor and mashing his head up against the cell roof. "If you're dead, you won't be able to use it."

Thornton's stranglehold around his collar was so tight, motes of light danced between them and Rattigan could draw in only a reedy breath. Blackness clawed at his vision, but then the pressure released when Thornton tossed him aside.

Rattigan slammed into the bars on the opposite side of the cell before sliding down them to lie in a heap on the floor. Thornton then loomed over him. Figuring that soon he'd be too weak to fight back, he flexed his shoulders and put all his strength into a manic charge.

He kicked off from the floor and, with his arms raised, he drove into Thornton's hips and shoved him across the cell. Thornton stepped backward until he walked into the bars, but he recovered quickly and hammered two bunched fists down on Rattigan's shoulders tearing him free.

Rattigan went to his knees where he

struggled to gather enough energy to move away from his opponent, but Thornton didn't take advantage of his weakened state, as behind him in the next cell, Warner had wrapped an arm around his neck through the bars.

"Give up or I tighten my grip," Warner said.

Thornton shook himself, but when he failed to dislodge Warner, he slumped and gave a brief nod. Warner held on to him until Rattigan had moved back to his cot. Then he withdrew his arm. Thornton stood for a while, seemingly weighing up his chances, until he smirked.

"Neither of us are going nowhere, and your friend can't protect you forever," he said.

Thornton feinted a lunge at Rattigan, making him draw his legs up. He laughed confidently at his reaction before he headed back to his cot. Rattigan murmured his thanks to Warner.

When he settled down, he figured his only hope was to ask the marshal to move him to another cell. As the other prisoners had barely reacted to the fight, he presumed such incidents were common.

So he had yet to think of a valid argument that might persuade Bishop to listen to him when the marshal returned to the jailhouse. Lurking behind him was Deputy Crane, who was shaking his head with his shoulders hunched. As he had done in the railroad office, Bishop paraded down the row of cells, ensuring he had everyone's attention.

"This morning I have eight prisoners," he said. "That's twice the number of bounty hunters who have collected information about Corbin Metz."

Bishop smiled, as if he expected them to work out what was on his mind, but the prisoners stood sullenly until Orville Grant spoke up. He was a burly overseer who had whipped one of his charges half to death with a knotted rope for going to sleep on the job.

"All we care about is seeing eight breakfasts," he said.

The prisoners laughed so Bishop raised a

bunch of keys. His confident demeanor killed off the laughter.

"You could enjoy those meals as free men."

"You've got our attention," Orville said.

"You can leave your cells, the crimes you've committed will be ignored and you can earn some easy money. All you have to do in return is one simple thing."

Bishop's offer was so surprising that nobody spoke as he walked back along the row of cells to join Crane. The deputy sighed before Bishop faced the prisoners, giving Rattigan a warning that the offer might not be as good as it had sounded so far.

"Bring in Corbin Metz," Bishop declared.

Derision broke the tension as the prisoners poured scorn on the offer. While Crane provided a knowing smile, everyone vied with each other to shout the loudest and to be the most scathing. Despite the cat-calling, Bishop maintained a disconcerting calmness that made the laughter die out.

"If you do this, you'll receive a share in the two-thousand-dollar bounty on Corbin's head," he said when he had quiet.

"If we were stupid enough to take that offer, we'd be the ones doing the dying," Orville said.

"If you don't take it, you're the stupid ones." Bishop chuckled. "Corbin has been killed. So you only have to bring in his dead body, and even you good-for-nothing varmints should be able to do that."

The cheer that erupted confirmed the prisoners thought so, too. The merriment soon spread to Thornton, who turned to Rattigan.

"The best thing about this mission is I'm sure to get an opportunity to kill you," he said with a grin.

* * *

"Stop feeling sorry for yourself," Sister Mary said after relating the result of her meeting with Marshal Bishop. "You only lost an arm."

"I lost more than that," Bradley said.

"The marshal said that although he was

grateful for what you did, the bounty would be paid to whoever brought in Corbin Metz. You didn't do that." Mary firmed her jaw as she failed to hide her disgust at Bradley's activities. "Although no doubt someone will rectify your failure soon."

"That won't be me. My partner's dead, and I'm half dead." With his lip curled in disgust Bradley gestured at his body using his left hand, but when Mary shook her head, he sighed, chiding himself for being relentlessly negative. "I'm obliged you told me the truth, but you can go now."

Bradley turned his head away making the sister mutter to herself. Then she came around the bed.

"Despite your disrespectful attitude," she declared, "you appear to be a resourceful man who'll cope with his new situation."

Bradley fingered his flattened jacket sleeve. "I was once a resourceful man. You made sure I'll never be that again."

"When I first examined you, your arm was already dead. We had to take it or by now you'd be dead, too. Even then, we still had to remove a bullet from your chest, and wounds like that are serious enough to kill most men. So be grateful for the gift our Lord has bestowed upon you."

"I'm trying," Bradley snapped.

She pursed her lips as she presumably reconsidered her approach, although unfortunately that resulted in her becoming more pious.

"With one good arm, there are many useful things you can do in the service of our Lord."

"I lost my right arm. I'm right-handed. When I got shot up, I was serving the Lord by tracking down a man for the bounty."

"As I told you, there are many *useful* things you can do."

Bradley forced a thin smile. "Name one."

Mary softened her expression from her usual scowl to a more benign frown.

"I don't know who saved your life. They placed you outside the mission door and left before we saw them. Finding them and conveying your gratitude would be a start."

Bradley had been nodding in a distracted

way, but Mary's final comment made him flinch.

"Whoever they are, they didn't claim the bounty," he mused.

When Mary didn't reply, Bradley flashed her a smile and settled down on his bed. Presently, she left him and, with no distractions, his mind raced. His two saviors didn't appear to have told Marshal Bishop about Corbin, so they might not have found his body.

Even better, they might have found it, but they hadn't known who he was and they'd buried him. If Corbin's body was no longer lying in the saloon in Red Creek, it would take whoever got there first to claim it a while to find out where it'd been buried.

So if he were lucky, he could still be the one who brought it back to Bear Rock. He also had a way to start his search as, when he'd been dragged out of the saloon, he had been sufficiently conscious to hear his saviors talking, and if he heard their voices again, he'd recognize them.

Calmer now, he accepted his situation

wasn't as hopeless as he'd first thought, but he could only rectify matters if he healed quickly. So for the first time since his accident, he examined his left hand and flexed the fingers as he wondered how effective the hand was.

"I don't know where you are, Corbin, but I hope you're rotting in hell," he said.

EIGHT

The high sun baked the man's body. His head throbbed and his right leg was pinned down. He pressed his hands to the ground for traction and shoved, but he didn't move. So he sat up and found that his predicament was a simple one.

His leg was trapped beneath a horse, and the enthusiastic flies reckoned it was a dead horse. He patted the steed's back, but he gathered no reaction so he put his hands to the withers. He was able to raise the shoulder for a few inches and that was enough to let him slide his leg away.

By degrees he edged his way clear. Once free, he rubbed his leg finding it jarred but otherwise in working order. Then he stood up, but that made pains announce themselves all over his body.

Every limb and every muscle ached, as if he'd been beaten badly. Worst of all, a bolt of pain shot from the back of his head to his forehead in a way that made him feel as if a vise was crushing his skull.

He doubled over, trying to relieve the pain, but that only made him vomit a thin stream of foam on to the ground and the retching set off a new encircling pain in his head. He clutched his temples and pressed.

The action didn't alleviate the pain, but it helped him to concentrate and, figuring that understanding his dilemma would help him, he moved on. While flexing his ankles and knees, he headed around the horse until he found the bloodied neck wound that confirmed the steed's fate.

High rocks loomed over him and he was standing in a clear area that was surrounded on three sides. So he turned to the entrance. Two men were lying on their backs thirty yards away.

Angry now, he shuffled over to the bodies and discovered that these men were as dead as the horse was. A rifle lay beside one man suggesting he'd shot the horse while a reddened patch on his chest showed he'd paid for his action.

The second man had been shot through the neck as well as in the side. Scuffed marks behind him showed he'd survived for long enough to drag himself through the dirt for a few yards toward the entrance. The blood on both men's bodies was damp.

"Who are you?" the man said.

He stood upright and he found that although his muscles still ached, the pain in his head had lessened, but he felt no joy as even more troubling thoughts assailed him. He couldn't remember why this gun battle had taken place, where he had been going, or where he'd come from.

As he wasn't carrying a gun, he couldn't even be sure he had shot the men. Then the most troubling question of all hit him, making him slap his forehead in frustration. His head rang like a bell and he swayed as the full horror of his failure to remember what had happened hit him.

"Who am I?" he said.

* * *

"You look like hell."

Bradley opened his eyes to find that Rattigan was his visitor.

"I feel like hell." Bradley forced himself to lie higher up on his bed. This movement was easier to make than it had been this morning and the small progress in his recovery cheered him. "So go away and let me suffer in peace."

"I have to leave quickly." Rattigan shrugged. "I got arrested."

"Then we both failed in our new lives as bounty hunters. What were you doing?"

"After you left town, I tried to work out why Corbin had returned to Bear Rock. Everything pointed to Victor knowing more than he'd let on about Marshal Dagwood's death, so I sneaked into the railroad office to see what I could find, but I had to escape through the window and I fell on Victor."

Bradley laughed for the first time in a

while. "I'd like to have seen that, but you don't look arrested now."

"The marshal cleared out the jailhouse to form a team of prisoners. To gain our freedom, we just have to collect Corbin's body from Red Creek."

Bradley tipped back his hat in bemusement. "I don't have much of a tale to tell. I didn't see our silver, so Corbin must have buried it elsewhere, and before the saloon collapsed in on us, Corbin claimed Victor killed the marshal, not him."

"I met Delano Metz and he claimed Victor did it, too." Rattigan pointed at Bradley's empty sleeve. "If we get to Corbin first, you can have my share of the bounty."

"I don't want your charity." Bradley grimaced as he strained to sit up straighter. "Although as you fail at everything, you'll probably fail to find Corbin."

"I'm glad I came." Rattigan uttered a rueful laugh. "At least I now know you're still as pig-headed as you ever were."

Bradley couldn't think of a withering retort. So he contented himself with an oath and turning his head away. Rattigan stood by his bed for a while, but when Bradley didn't turn back, he patted the bed and headed to the door.

Only when Sister Mary chastised Rattigan for having stayed too long did he try to get comfortable on the bed. The movement made an object nudge his hip. He found that when Rattigan had patted the bed he had in fact deposited Bradley's Colt.

Bradley smiled. Yesterday, while he'd been unconscious, Mary had taken his gun. Since then, she'd rebuffed his requests for her to give it back.

"Perhaps you're not a failure, after all, Rattigan," he said to himself as he slipped the gun from view.

After rummaging around awkwardly with his left hand, he slotted the weapon into a fold of the sheet where he reckoned Mary wouldn't find it. Then he settled down for what he hoped would be a quiet afternoon. He judged that an hour had passed when Mary spoke up from the other side of the door.

"He's had as many visitors as he can cope with today," she declared.

The angry grunt and the scuffing feet said that his visitor had taken the unwise move of ignoring the nun. Bradley considered locating the gun, but he didn't want Mary to find out he'd defied her yet, so he leaned on his left elbow to face the door. He wished he'd gone for the gun instead when Victor came in followed by Mary and six other railroad men.

"I've heard a rumor you killed Corbin," Victor said. "You'll tell me the truth."

While Victor's companions spread out around the room, Mary stood between Victor and Bradley. Her scowl promised that she would cut this meeting short if Bradley asked her to.

"There's not much to tell," Bradley said. "Percy and me found Corbin holed up in Red Creek. My partner was shot to pieces and so was I."

"Tell me the important part of this story."

"Corbin died before I could find out where he hid the silver, but I don't reckon—"

"I don't care about the silver. The only thing I care about is seeing Corbin's lifeless body."

Bradley shook his head. "I barely got out of Red Creek alive. I wasn't fit enough to bring his body with me."

Victor moved for the door, making Mary head across the room to follow him out, but instead Victor shoved the door shut. Then the other two men headed to Bradley's bed.

"You'll leave now," Mary shouted after them. "This man is—"

She was cut off when one of Victor's men moved in and slapped a hand over her mouth. Then he swung her around to hold her from behind. Bradley rummaged beneath his sheet for his gun, but he acted too slowly.

One man grabbed his legs and he was too weak to stop him swinging them off the bed while the other man went behind him and levered him up to a sitting position. Since he'd woken up in the mission, he had been encouraged to stand up several times, but for only short periods.

So when he was pushed out of bed, he could only stand hunched over and he reckoned he'd struggle to get back to the bed without help. Victor walked up to him. Bradley raised his head for as far as he was able, which was level with Victor's chin.

By the door Mary was struggling, but she was being held tightly. Victor clicked his fingers and the two men who had moved him off the bed closed ranks behind him.

"You'll now tell me your story again," Victor said. "You'll start from the moment I found you loitering near Delano Metz's house. This time you'll leave nothing out, or this will happen."

He stepped in and thudded a punch into Bradley's side. Thankfully, Victor hit him on the opposite side to his gunshot wound, but it still made pain slice through his chest. Unable to control his motion, he reeled backward until the men behind stilled him and then shoved him forward.

"You have no reason to hit me," Bradley said between gasps. "I went after Corbin and I killed him."

"If you'd told the truth, I'd have no reason, but as you lied. . . ."

Victor raised a fist, but he didn't hit him again so in short bursts Bradley retold his story. This time he related how he'd followed wheel ruts, although he didn't say they had originated at Delano's house. Then he recalled his exchange with Corbin, leaving out the claim that Victor had killed the marshal, in the hope that something he had said would placate Victor.

"So I left him lying in the dry creek," he said, finishing his tale with a defiant lie. "Then I came here to get fixed up."

Victor appraised Bradley's battered form. "I'd have believed you if you hadn't ended your story with such an obvious lie. You can barely stand, never mind make the journey from Red Creek."

Bradley raised his left hand and gestured at where his right hand would have been.

"Look at me. It's yet to be decided if I survived."

"That's the first thing you've said that I do believe."

Victor sneered giving Bradley enough time to tense before he delivered a punch to his cheek that cracked his head to the left followed by a backhanded slap that knocked his head to the right. Before Bradley could recover, one of the men standing behind him thudded a low punch into his kidneys that sent him to his knees.

Then the other man raised a boot and pressed it against his back. A light shove tipped him over. He kept enough presence of mind to ensure he fell gently on his wounded side, but that left the stump of his right arm uppermost.

Victor jabbed two quick kicks into his stomach, but the third kick caught his stump, making him screech in agony. He slumped over on to his back and writhed as bolts of hot pain cascaded up and down an arm that was no longer there.

Through the waves of pain, he heard Mary's strident voice demanding that Victor leave. Then a scuffle broke out, but even the possibility that the nun was being assaulted couldn't help him gather control.

He was still whimpering when he was dragged to his feet. He didn't have enough strength to keep his head raised so one of his assailants tugged his hair forcing him to face Victor. Behind Victor, two men were now holding Mary while one man wedged the door closed with his foot, presumably keeping the other nuns from entering.

"I told the truth," Bradley said through gritted teeth as he struggled to stay conscious. "I killed Corbin."

"Give me one reason to believe you," Victor said.

Victor slapped a hand on his right shoulder and a bolt of pain transfixed his stump and made him feel that his non-existent hand was on fire.

"Marshal Bishop believed me," he screeched, desperate to please his tormentor. "He cleared out the jailhouse and formed a band of prisoners, including my brother, to collect his body."

Victor flinched and Bradley's captors released him, letting him drop to the floor. Bradley expected the beating would resume, and he knew he'd tell Victor anything to make him stop, but they stepped over him and headed to the door.

"You've been most hospitable, Sister Mary," Victor said with mock courtesy.

"You've been most unpleasant, but I'll still pray for you," Mary said.

"If you pray for anything, pray I have Corbin's body before sundown tomorrow." Victor smirked. "If I don't, I'll return."

Victor moved on. The moment the door was released two nuns spilled inside, but after a nod from Mary, they backed away letting the men leave. Then the sisters hurried across the room to help Bradley back on to the bed. He let them aid him without complaint.

"I commend you for not reacting aggress-ively to those men's unacceptable behavior," Mary said, coming over to him.

Bradley lay back on his bed and with deep, racking breaths he willed the pain to recede. His movements made the cold gun press into the back of his thigh. He entertained the thought of chasing after Victor and making him pay for what he'd done, but when the pain in his phantom arm made tears spring to his eyes, he had to dismiss the possibility.

"I had no choice," Bradley said, the admittance hurting him more than the beating had. "I'm only half a man."

NINE

"Did your brother tell you anything interesting?" Marshal Bishop asked when he and Rattigan joined the straggling procession of riders a mile past Dead Man's Canyon.

The marshal had taken charge of the eight unarmed prisoners to ensure they carried out their side of the deal. While Rattigan had talked with Bradley, Bishop had waited for him, but he had let the prisoners ride on ahead alone, presumably giving them leeway as a test to see how much he could trust his new charges. As Rattigan counted seven riders, that test had succeeded.

"Nothing that'll help us claim Corbin's body any quicker," Rattigan said. He shrugged when Bishop narrowed his eyes. "My brother wasn't a talkative man when he was fit, and his injuries haven't made him any more sociable."

"I'd gathered from our meeting in the railroad office that he wasn't an easy man to talk to, but if you're holding out on me, you won't get nothing out of this other than a return to your jail cell."

Rattigan raised a hand to shoulder level in a mime of surrendering.

"In that case don't blame me for this, but apparently before he died, Corbin claimed that Victor Greystone killed Marshal Dagwood."

Bishop accepted his statement with a scowl, but Rattigan reckoned he didn't look surprised and he didn't question him anymore before he moved on to lead the riders. As he passed the men, he formed them into a tight-knit formation.

For the rest of the afternoon they rode at a steady mile-eating pace without incident, but as they'd set off too late to reach Red Creek today, when the sun lowered they made camp. While they settled down, Rattigan ensured he stayed away from

Thornton and stayed close to Warner, but the sun had yet to set when the arguing started.

Everyone had a loud and different view about the position of the camp, how big a fire they should make and what they would eat. Bishop let the bickering run on, presumably to let the prisoners work out their differences.

When it showed no sign of ending, he let out an exasperated roar of anger. Then, when everyone had quieted, he walked into the center of the camp.

"You've been released from jail without charge," he declared. "All you have to do in return is collect a body, and you'll get a share in a two-thousand-dollar bounty. You have no reason to argue."

The reminder of the money made everyone nod and, with a few grumbles at a lower volume, they settled down around the fire.

"How will we split the money?" Orville asked after a while.

"There are nine of us," Warner said. "So I say we split it evenly. That's over two hundred dollars each."

"There are eight of you," Bishop said with a weary air. "I'm a lawman. I won't gain from this."

If the marshal had expected a sympathetic response, he'd have been disappointed as his misfortune gathered only smirks.

"If we're unlucky not all of us will make it back to Bear Rock," Thornton said. "So those that do will get even more money each."

"Then let's hope you're one of the ones who gets lost on the way," Rattigan said.

Thornton glowered while the rest of the group laughed and, with a potential new argument about to flare up, Bishop shook his head sadly and moved over to tend to the fire. Thornton took the opportunity to head around the fire and hunker down beside Rattigan. With the other prisoners looking on eagerly expecting trouble, Rattigan tensed while Warner got up on his haunches ready to act.

"You're a funny man," Thornton said loudly with apparent good humor. When his comment made the prisoners shrug, he lowered his voice for Rattigan's ears only. "You're not provoking me into acting openly."

"I have no interest in provoking you at all."

"It's too late for that. At some point on this journey your friends won't be close by and then I'll take my chances."

Thornton rocked forward and feinted a punch at him, but unlike in the cell this morning Rattigan didn't jerk away. Thornton gave a wide smile before returning to his former position.

Bishop wasn't looking their way and, when he finished with the fire, he picked his way through the men to stand alone and face the route they'd take tomorrow. Rattigan joined him. He stood beside the marshal for a minute composing his words before he turned to him.

"I'd broken into the railroad office when you and Victor came upstairs," he said. "I tried to escape through the window, but I fell and Victor broke my fall."

Bishop raised an eyebrow with an unconcerned expression that said he'd already worked this out.

"I'm obliged you've admitted that, but it proves Victor was right to want you locked away for a good many years."

In the camp everyone had resorted to surly silence. Only Thornton was paying attention to them, but he wasn't near enough to hear him.

"As you suspected that already, why are you letting me earn an amnesty with these men?"

Bishop waved a dismissive hand at the prisoners.

"If I'd released you without charge, Victor would have asked too many difficult questions, but I reckon I can justify a mass amnesty." Bishop smiled. "I'd hoped that on the way, you'd be so grateful you'd tell me what you found out in the railroad office."

Rattigan returned the smile. "I found nothing. When I got into the office, the safe was already open and empty."

Bishop searched his eyes, presumably

wondering if he were keeping something back, and Rattigan hoped he didn't force him to betray Delano.

"So someone got there before you, which must mean there was something worth knowing, perhaps even proof that your brother was right and Victor did kill Marshal Dagwood, not Corbin."

A raised voice sounded behind them and they turned to find that a new argument was breaking out between Orville and Thornton. Rattigan lowered his head and kicked at the dirt before he sighed.

"Without that information and with Corbin dead, I guess that'll probably be impossible to prove," he said.

* * *

"How did you find your gun?" Sister Mary said. "I hid it well."

"Not well enough," Bradley said.

He took aim at the tin can and fired. Although he was only thirty feet away, a puff of dust rose up eight feet to the side of the can having taken a trajectory that was four feet above it.

"You didn't fire well enough. I'm relieved I'm standing behind you."

Bradley couldn't argue with that. The revolver had served him well, but he'd never been called upon to use his left hand. He was still so battered and sore he had to stand hunched over and he favored his injured side.

Worse, since he'd dragged himself out of bed, being mobile reminded him that not all of him was there anymore. Every movement he made somehow required him to use his non-existent right hand, giving him a nagging reminder of his crippled state.

"With my aim being this bad, I'm relieved I'm standing behind the gun, too."

"Then throw it away. You don't need it."

Bradley shuffled around to face her. Then he lowered the gun and moved as if to chuck it aside.

"Perhaps I will." He waited until she nodded approvingly. "But only after I've collected my bounty. Until then, I'll keep practicing to make sure I can defend us when Victor returns."

He started to raise the gun while turning back to the can, but she spoke loudly making him lower it.

"If you didn't carry a gun, you wouldn't have to defend us." She raised the cross that she wore around her neck. "This provides better protection than any weapon."

"That wouldn't work for me."

"It could." She held out a hand for the gun. "The first step will be to stop relying on the power of your gun; that'll let you put faith in the strength of your mind."

"I'm obliged for your advice. Perhaps I should stop shooting and start thinking." Bradley smiled. "I'll start by doing what you advised earlier and track down the men who found me."

"I approve of your plan." Her tone was less irritated than it usually was, but she still cast an aggrieved look at his gun.

"I'll leave tomorrow." He holstered his gun and stretched, but the action made him feel light-headed and he stumbled to the right.

"Then again, perhaps I'll wait until the day after that."

"Nonsense. You'll be fit enough to leave in the morning, with my help, of course."

"You want to help me?" Bradley spluttered.

"You aren't fit enough to sit a horse yet, but I'll take you to wherever you want to go."

Bradley waved his left arm as he struggled to find the right response.

"Why would you want to do that?" he said.

"Because news of your return has gotten out and others are now looking for the body of this poor dead man. Questioning the men who found you is probably your only chance of finding him first, so you can't delay or you'll never get your one-thousand-dollar bounty."

Bradley narrowed his eyes. "The bounty's two thousand dollars."

She frowned. "Your grasp of numbers is clearly as poor as your aim. I've divided the two thousand evenly between you and me."

Bradley raised an incredulous eyebrow. "I thought nuns weren't interested in money?"

"We're not, but the hospital I run is, and I can put the money to good use. Now, you need to stop tiring yourself out shooting up defenseless rocks and rest. We'll leave one hour after sunup tomorrow."

"I can be ready at sunup."

"You won't." She took his left arm and guided him back to the mission. "You'll spend that hour in prayer seeking the strength of mind to leave your gun behind."

TEN

The man had lost all track of time, but he still trudged on. He kept the high rocks to his right and forced himself to place one foot in front of the other, all without any hope that he would reach somewhere before his strength gave out.

The low sun was throwing out his long and diffuse shadow before him when the tracks he was following led to a house. The sight lightened his step and he rubbed his forehead, as if by rubbing he might force himself to remember something about a past that remained as blank as the feature-less plains to his left.

The action only made his head throb again, but with the pain being less debilit-ating than it had been when he'd woken up, he located the sorest spot as being on the back of his head. Here matted and damp hair covered a bump that was too sore to withstand anything other than a light touch.

He had followed his horse's tracks assuming he would fetch up in the place he'd left. His pounding head, his battered limbs and his confused state caused by his failure to recall even simple facts such as his own name meant that his progress had been slow, and he judged that he'd covered only three miles.

The house was familiar, although he could summon up no memories other than a vague sense that he knew the place. The barn in particular felt like somewhere he'd visited before and he moved on, speeding up to a trot now that answers to his many questions could be imminent.

When he reached the barn, he ran his fingers along the wooden wall, hoping the rough texture would rekindle a memory. It didn't and he shuffled along the wall to the open double-doors. Beyond was only a darkened interior.

"So you returned," a man said behind him.

He turned, and the sudden action made his vision swirl forcing him to grip the barn door with both hands. When he was able to focus, the speaker was standing in the doorway to the house.

This man was as familiar as the barn and house were and yet, like those buildings, he had no idea why he was familiar. The confusion made him sway. Then nausea burned his throat, but there was nothing left in his stomach to vomit so this time he fought down the feeling with a determined gulp.

"I had nowhere else to go," he said.

"That's not a good enough answer."

The man took a deep breath to gather his strength before he set off for the house. At the door he stomped to a halt and stood hunched over. The owner's features were no more familiar than before so he dropped to his knees.

"Who am I?" he beseeched.

The owner frowned. "So you still claim you can't remember nothing?"

Despite the disappointing answer, the

man smiled, pleased that at least he'd returned to the right place and hopefully to someone who could help him.

"I can't remember nothing, not my name, not this place, not my reason for being here, nothing." The man placed his hands together in an attitude of prayer. "Tell me, please, who I am."

"I won't tell you. You need to remember it for yourself and, if your need is great enough, you will." His tone was strained, as if they'd had this conversation before. "Otherwise, you'll live the rest of your life without a past not knowing whether you're a decent man or an outlaw. So think, and think harder than you've ever thought before."

The man closed his eyes and delved into the black hole of his past that contained only his journey away from the dead horse and the dead men. Then, from somewhere, a name slipped into his mind.

"Delano Metz?" he said, opening his eyes.

This suggestion gathered a frown followed by an encouraging smile.

"So you've finally remembered *my* name. That's a start." He came forward and drew the man to his feet. "Now let's see what else you can remember."

"Nothing, other than that two dead men are lying out there," the man said, pointing.

"Who are they?" Delano said.

The man shook his head, an action he regretted when it made his forehead throb.

"I don't know."

"Do you remember killing them?"

"I told you. I can't remember nothing." The man shrugged. "I don't reckon I'm the kind of man who could have done it."

Having made the declaration, his heart thudded with assurance and he walked into the house, hoping his confidence would help him to remember more. It failed and he turned to find that Delano had followed him and he was standing up close.

Anger had contorted Delano's face so the man hurried outside, but Delano advanced on him forcing the man to quicken. His foot turned on a rock making him stumble and Delano unbalanced him by pushing his chest.

He landed on his rump where he sat with his head aching while Delano stood over him. Then he had to turn away as the light from the setting sun burned into his eyes.

"Look at me," Delano said, his fists clenching. "Tell me the names of those two men."

"You can't force me to remember with threats. All I can remember is I was lying trapped beneath a dead horse and two dead men were nearby. They'd been shot and I didn't have a gun." The man raised his eyes for as far as he could while still avoiding the sun. "You're wearing a six-shooter."

Delano snorted with anger and dragged the man to his feet.

"You can't avoid the truth with insinuations. Remember, damn you."

The man turned to the barn, but the sudden movement disorientated him. When his vision had stopped swirling, he still didn't feel guilty.

"I can't, but I do know one thing. I didn't kill those men."

"Someone did," Delano said. Then he

131

thudded a low punch into the man's stomach that made him drop to his knees.

The man dragged in harsh breaths that failed to relieve the pain forcing him to rock forward until his forehead touched the ground.

"Why did you do that?" he bleated.

"Because I know the truth about what you've done," Delano roared, "and no brother of mine can escape justice by forgetting his past!"

The man raised his head, finding that he stood in Delano's shadow. His vision was blurred and his head felt like it was about to split in two, but he'd heard Delano's mistake.

"You just told me something," he gasped. "I'm your brother."

Delano slapped a hand to his forehead, confirming that revealing this detail had been a mistake.

"You are, so remember the rest."

The man closed his eyes and he considered names, searching for one that sounded as if it should accompany his given name of

Metz. He smiled and opened his eyes.

"Corbin Metz?" he said.

Delano held out his hand to help the man to his feet.

"That's your name," he declared.

"I'm Corbin Metz!" the man shouted happy beyond all reason to have dragged another piece of his hidden past into his uncertain present.

Delano scowled. Then he punched him on the nose sending him reeling before he tumbled over to lie on his side. Delano loomed over him and tapped the toe of his boot on the ground with an insistent rhythm.

"So now that you know who you are, you can pay the price for your crimes," he said with relish.

Then Delano kicked him in the stomach.

ELEVEN

Red Creek was as deserted as it had been the first time Rattigan had passed through. Despite the bickering last night, this morning the prisoners had been quiet with everyone appearing eager to complete the task.

So, as the ghost town opened up to them, the lead riders moved on, which encouraged those behind to speed up to get ahead of them. Marshal Bishop didn't curtail their enthusiasm and the riders surged into town at a gallop, but Rattigan stayed back with the marshal.

Everyone dismounted. Then they ran around with plenty of chaotic activity that failed to locate the saloon from among the dozens of ruined and collapsed buildings. By the time he and Bishop trotted into town, everyone was waiting for them and for the first time they turned to the marshal for guidance. Bishop stopped beside Bradley and Rattigan's abandoned wagon.

"The saloon is the first building you come across from this direction," Bishop said, pointing.

He didn't need to add any more as the prisoners hurried to the indicated building where in an uncoordinated manner they hurled planks aside as they sought to burrow their way inside. Rattigan and Bishop dismounted and then stood back.

"I'm not volunteering for this," Rattigan said when Bishop turned to him. "This is sure to be gruesome."

"It might not be," Bishop said in a distracted way as he turned to the empty wagon. "I don't reckon they'll find Corbin. This morning I found recent tracks. Several riders must have passed us in the night, and I assume they'll include Victor."

"Did you tell him about our mission?"

"No, but he has a way of finding things out and he'll be desperate to get to Corbin first."

By now the men were crawling into the

wrecked saloon along the triangular space left by a wall that supported a length of fallen ceiling. Rattigan presumed this path had been used to free Bradley. Five minutes later, Thornton emerged from the saloon with the rest of the prisoners trailing behind and came over shaking his head.

"Nothing," he said, setting his hands on his hips.

"You didn't search for long," Bishop said.

"We looked for long enough." Thornton sniffed. "If a body was there, we'd be able to tell."

"Nobody's claimed the bounty yet so it's possible someone found him who didn't know what he was worth and they buried him."

Orville nodded and gathered the prisoners around him, but with the former overseer apparently eager to revert to his old supervising role, the marshal gestured at Warner.

"Make sure these men search all the likely burial sites in and around town," he said. "I'll scout around with Rattigan."

Warner straightened his back in surprise

as the marshal drew a distinction in their statuses while Thornton joined Orville in glowering at Bishop's chosen man. Despite their antipathy, Warner confidently delivered orders leaving Bishop and Rattigan to head away.

"I assume you don't want them to know that Victor might have found him?" Rattigan said when they'd moved out of earshot.

"Not until we know for sure."

Rattigan nodded. Then, while the prisoners spread out and searched the northern edge of town, they examined the southern buildings. A fire had raged on this side of town, converting the buildings into blackened husks that weren't substantial enough to hide Victor, so Rattigan turned to the rising land to the east while Bishop faced the bend of the dry wash a hundred yards away.

Bishop directed them to split up. When the marshal moved off, Rattigan headed between two ravaged buildings. He came out on the other side and craned his neck, but he faced a still scene that didn't give him the feeling that Victor was on this side of town.

He turned away planning to find out how Bishop was faring, but a crunched footfall close by alerted him. He stepped aside and avoided a swiping blow from a heavy plank that Thornton had aimed at his head, which if it had connected would have knocked him senseless.

Even so, the wind created by the blow rustled past his cheek and the force used unbalanced Thornton. The plank slammed down into the ground with a resounding thud that tore it from his hands.

Thornton grunted with anger as he reclaimed the plank, but before he could raise it, Rattigan saw where Thornton had found his weapon and he hurried to a pile of old planks that were propped up against a foreshortened wall. With Thornton closing in on him quickly, he picked up the nearest plank and swung around with it held two-handed before his chest.

Thornton tried the same tactic as before of swinging the plank down at his head, but this time it met the shield Rattigan had held up. Thornton's plank snapped, but that didn't deter him and he jabbed the short length of wood at Rattigan's stomach.

With a downward swing of his plank Rattigan parried the wood aside. When Thornton's momentum bent him double, Rattigan shoved the top of his plank forward, clipping Thornton's chin and sending him to his knees.

Rattigan wasted no time in carrying out the action Thornton had tried by raising his plank high and dashing it down over his assailant's head. At the last moment Thornton jerked aside and took most of the blow on his shoulders, but it was still strong enough to shatter the plank and knock him on to his side.

Rattigan then picked up a more solid looking plank and held it aloft. He enjoyed himself by making a feint that made Thornton scramble away rapidly. Then he moved in purposefully aiming to make the next blow decisive.

"Where are you?" Warner called from the

other side of the building. "We've found a grave."

Marshal Bishop shouted a reply. He was too far away for Rattigan to hear what he said, but the interruption let his anger dissipate. He stood over Thornton, his weapon held casually.

"My friends weren't nearby and you took your chance," he said. "You failed."

"You got lucky," Thornton said. He got up on to one knee, although he did so groggily making his taunt a hollow one.

"I intend to stay lucky." Rattigan tossed the plank aside. "If you want to stay lucky, too, keep out of my way."

He headed through the gap between the buildings. He found Warner directing Marshal Bishop to a spot on the other side of town. Then Warner scampered off leaving Bishop to walk back with him. Bishop smiled, as if he knew what had just happened.

"I saw Victor," Bishop said, pointing at the wash.

"Searching for Corbin's body or for the

silver?"

"If what I suspect is true, Victor will only be interested in confirming that Corbin is dead."

Rattigan nodded. Then they followed Warner to the indicated spot, where Orville was standing beside a shallow grave sporting a sour expression. The rest of the men who had helped him dig were shaking their heads.

"It's not Corbin," Orville said.

While Bishop moved on to investigate the grave, Thornton arrived. He didn't meet Rattigan's eye.

"That's Percy Jedson," Bishop said when he reached the hole. "He was one of the bounty hunters who went after Corbin."

Orville shrugged. "So why did someone bury him, but not Corbin?"

Bishop beckoned everyone to form a line, making the prisoners scowl and mutter, this discovery having destroyed their enthusiasm.

"This mission's become harder than I expected, but if we keep cool heads, we'll still find Corbin," he said when he had quiet.

"That's not what's worrying us," Orville said. "There's no body and that must mean the bounty hunter got it wrong. Corbin is still alive."

The suggestion made everyone frown with mounting worry.

"It's unlikely, but that's not your concern. You're prisoners and if you want to stay out of jail, you have a task to complete."

"I have a better idea." Orville took a step forward. He placed one hand on his hip while he held the other behind his back. "We forget about Corbin and we search for the missing silver instead."

"You're not doing that."

Orville smirked, making Rattigan gulp with concern when most of the men sneered at Bishop.

"It seems we will," Orville said. "I reckon six of us say we want to find the silver, not Corbin."

"Then I'll escort those six back to jail."

Bishop directed the prisoners to head back to their horses. The men folded their arms so Bishop moved toward Thornton. He'd taken a single step when Orville jerked the arm he'd held behind his back into view, and clutched in his hand was a gun.

Rattigan just had enough time to register that Percy must have been buried with his weapon when Orville fired. His shot tore into Bishop's stomach making the marshal fold over and stagger forward for a pace.

With a pained grunt, Bishop righted himself and reached for his gun. He had yet to touch it when a second shot to the forehead downed him.

"I don't reckon we're following your orders now," Orville said with a smirk as Bishop slumped down on his back, lifeless.

For long moments nobody moved, everyone seemingly as surprised as Bishop had been that Orville had gotten his hands on a gun.

"You've made us all into outlaws," Warner said, aghast.

"We were already outlaws."

"Some of us had only been dragged in for that saloon fight."

"That doesn't matter now. You have a choice. You either join me, or you don't."

Orville left the threat unsaid of what would happen if they chose the latter, but while everyone waited to see what the majority would do, Rattigan made his decision. He hurried to Bishop's side and moved to claim his gun.

He didn't even lay a finger on it as Thornton stepped forward and kicked out. His boot clipped Rattigan's chin and sent him reeling on to his back. Then Thornton slapped a hand on the weapon.

"I'm with you," he said hefting the gun.

Thornton's decision made others speak up to pledge their allegiance to Orville. Within moments, the only people not to join him were Warner and Rattigan.

"So it'd seem you're the only ones not going after the silver," Orville said with a grin.

"They still have one last task," Thornton said. He pointed at a spot beside Percy's grave. "They can dig three graves. Then I'll fill them."

TWELVE

"Please leave me alone," Corbin said when Delano came for him in the morning. "I still don't know what you want of me."

Delano stood framed in the doorway to the barn regarding his brother with a mixture of disappointment and anger in his eyes. Worryingly, he'd looped a coil of rope over a shoulder.

"Remembering your crimes will be a start," Delano said.

"I can't remember anything more today."

"Then this day will be an even longer day for you than yesterday was." Delano came in and dragged Corbin to his feet.

Yesterday Delano had beaten him with his fists. When he'd tired, he'd used a cudgel. All the time he'd inflicted the punishment with grim determination and no amount of pleading could make him stop.

Corbin didn't know what had made Delano's anger erupt after he'd remembered his name; he had thought this recollection would please him. When Delano had become too exhausted to inflict more harm on him, he'd sat on the stoop while Corbin had lain in a bruised and bloodied heap on the ground.

With his feet resting on the porch fence, he'd leaned back in his chair and eaten a heel of bread while supping water messily, reinforcing the fact he wasn't going to feed or water him. Then he'd locked him in the barn, but even if the door had been unlocked, Corbin had been too weary and sore to try to get away and he'd suffered a long night failing to find a comfortable way to lie.

Today, his past was still a blank, and even the names he'd recalled no longer felt as right as they had done when he'd first remembered them. This time, Delano walked him out of the barn and around the house to a fenced-off area.

When Delano had taken him through a gate, he deposited him before a rectangular hole with a stake set before it. Corbin tensed when he recognized the hole as being a grave.

"Is this where it ends?" he asked as Delano tipped the coil of rope off his shoulder.

Delano sneered, as if this question was the worst one he could have asked, before he played out the rope. Corbin was too exhausted to object when he looped the end around his chest.

When Delano had wrapped three coils around him, he tugged him to his feet and stood him up against the stake. His arms were dragged back and another three loops secured him before Delano stood back.

Corbin reckoned that even if the rope were loose, he was too weak to escape. In fact, as he couldn't avoid slumping forward, the rope was the only thing keeping him upright.

"Does this hole stir up any memories yet?"

Delano asked.

"None," Corbin said, facing the empty grave.

"Something terrible happened here." Delano pointed at the grave. "You'll stay here looking into this hole until you remember what it is."

The abyss seemed to draw him forward and his weakness along with the pain in his head unfocused his eyes. He fought off the dizzy feeling with determined deep breaths and then forced his head up, but Delano remained a fuzzy blur.

"I can't do this. If I'm to remember, I need your help."

Delano snarled, but he went to the other end of the grave where he picked up an old wooden cross. He brought it over and thrust it up before Corbin's face. Writing was on the small cross, but the mildew and rot that obscured the names would have made them hard to discern even if he wasn't having trouble focusing.

"Estelle and Malachi," Delano said.

"Are they our parents?" Corbin guessed,

relying on the age of the cross.

"Yes. Once, they lay here at peace, but no longer."

Corbin blinked rapidly, sharpening Delano's stern visage.

"Are you saying someone . . . *I* dug them up?"

"You've committed many terrible acts in that life you can no longer remember, but that was the worst."

Corbin shook his head. "I can't believe I'd do that."

Delano raised head and roared with anger before throwing the cross down into the grave.

"You stole silver in Bear Rock and shot up a heap of men," he said, speaking quickly. "You came here and dug up our parents' grave. You discarded their bodies before burying the silver in a coffin here."

Corbin furrowed his brow. "The silver's not here now."

"I know." Delano turned to him with his fists bunched, his expression more eager than at any time during his interrogation.

"So what happened to the silver after you buried it?"

"I don't know." Corbin closed his eyes and tried to imagine the situation that Delano had described, but he couldn't make the images form and he couldn't believe he would do such a thing. "I just don't know."

Delano walked up to him and slapped his cheek, the blow a caress after the earlier punishment. Corbin braced himself for worse, but Delano's eyes were troubled, as if the slap had been the strongest one he could inflict. Then he winced and stepped back while feeling the back of his head.

"Remember, damn you," he murmured, his tone weary.

Delano bent over and placed a hand on his knee while he removed his hat to mop his brow. The movement revealed matted blood on the side of his head and a livid bruise on his neck.

"You've been hurt, too," Corbin said.

"These last few days, we've both faced tough situations," Delano said, his voice kindly for the first time since he'd become angry.

His softer tone and his apparent distress made Corbin stop worrying about trying to remember. Then, almost as if all he had to do to remember was to let go of the need, he pictured something he hadn't recalled before, something that had happened before he'd lost his name. He was being beaten by a man, his form just an outline in the darkness, and he repeated a familiar demand.

"A man beat me," he said. "He demanded to know where I'd hidden the silver."

"Did you talk?" Delano asked.

"I said nothing. So the beating continued. I got hit on the head. I passed out. The next I knew I was lying out there under a dead horse."

Delano smiled. "Who was the man?"

"I didn't see his face, but the more important thing is that when we work together, we uncover more than when you hurt me."

"Then remember what happened after you buried the silver but before this man beat you." Delano stood tall and pointed at the grave. "Perhaps you dug up the silver and took it farther up Dead Man's Canyon?"

"I've told you: I don't know. I don't know!" Corbin shouted his answer until he became too hoarse to continue. Then he slumped against his bonds, his breath coming in harsh gasps.

Delano walked up to him and again he slapped his cheek. Then he walked around the stake to stand behind him.

"Remember," he whispered in his ear.

His urgent tone made another memory form of his earlier tormentor whispering that same command. Corbin gulped.

"I know who beat me now," he said, his voice small. "It was *you*. You hit me until I lost my memory and now you're beating me again."

"I sure am, and you'll stay here until you can remember the rest."

"That means you don't care about justice, or about revenge for what I did to our parents' bodies. This has all been about one thing: you want that silver for yourself."

Delano grunted an oath and kicked the stake. It creaked and toppled, sending

Corbin rocking forward toward the open grave. As the stake swung down Corbin tensed, but the top of the stake crunched down beyond the grave, stopping him short of the bottom of the hole.

Delano then walked away, leaving him dangling in the grave like a hog-tied carcass spitted over a fire. The gate creaked shut. Then his only company was the grave dirt below.

* * *

"I prayed you wouldn't bring your gun today," Sister Mary said when she came out of the chapel.

She hadn't let Bradley pray with the other nuns in the small chapel. So he'd sat outside with his head lowered to await a journey he'd gladly not take.

"I prayed I wouldn't have to use it," Bradley said.

As they headed to the small open wagon, Mary favored Bradley with a thin-lipped smile at his seeming partial acquiescence. In truth he had meant that if a tough situation arose, he didn't feel fit enough to use it.

"You should ride on the back," Mary said when they reached the wagon.

"I'm not lying on the back like a cripple," Bradley said. "I'll sit on the seat with you."

"In that case, I'll use our journey to discuss the fate of your immortal soul."

Bradley winced. "I'll take the back."

He shuffled to the back of the wagon where, after several hops to test his strength, he jumped while twisting. This let him land on the edge. Sadly, he then found that walking from the mission and getting on the wagon had exhausted him.

So he crawled along the base to flop down with his head rested on a folded sack. As Mary took the wagon away from the mission and then swung around to the east, Bradley tried to roll with the swaying, but every movement jolted him.

He sat up, but that action required several clawed movements using his left hand and they used up every last reserve of strength. So he sat slumped over and feeling wretched about his lack of agility, strength and fortitude.

He had hoped he would feel a little better each day, but today he felt as weak as he had done yesterday and he wished he were back in the mission lying on his bed. With Victor and others searching for Corbin's body, the likelihood of him getting ahead of them felt remote, but Mary appeared optimistic.

When they arrived in Bear Rock, she wasted no time before she started a systematic investigation. Outside the first building she came to, she alighted and questioned the first man who wasn't quick enough to get out of her way. She didn't call on Bradley's help.

"Do you know that man?" she asked, gesturing at the wagon and, as she might be trying to elicit sympathy, Bradley dangled his empty jacket sleeve over the side of the wagon.

"I'm afraid I don't," the man said while cringing, apparently expecting retribution after failing to please her.

"Do you know of anyone visiting Red

Creek in the last two days?" As the man was shaking his head vigorously, she paused and glowered at him until he stilled. "Do you know of anyone going to the mission with an injured man?"

"I surely don't," the man said with a sigh that suggested he wished he were elsewhere. "That's a place I never want to go to."

Mary set her hands on her hips. "You don't know much about anything, do you?"

"I try not to. Can I go now?"

"Only after you promise to come and find me if, by some heaven-sent miracle, you happen to stumble across acceptable answers to my questions."

The man nodded eagerly, and when she moved aside, he scampered off leaving Mary to go in search of the next unfortunate who didn't see her coming. With her directing her withering scowls at others, Bradley couldn't help but appreciate her vigor, although the frantic headshakes that followed her every question didn't give him hope that she'd succeed.

The failures didn't dampen her spirit, and

when she reached the end of the main drag, she worked her way back down the other side. Most of the town's saloons were here and Bradley was amused when she didn't venture into any of them. So he had started rehearsing an argument for him to take over the questioning inside these buildings when her persistence was rewarded in a mercantile.

"The men who saved you could be merchants," she said, coming over to the side of the wagon. "Apparently two men often go through Red Creek and they're several days late with a delivery."

"I'm impressed. The church's gain is bounty hunting's loss." Bradley chuckled when she narrowed her eyes. "Did you find out where they are now?"

"They were last seen near Dead Man's Canyon, presumably after leaving you at the mission." She clambered up on to the seat and turned to him in the back. "Do you have any ideas where they might have gone?"

"I don't, but I guess I could have talked in my sleep about Corbin." Bradley rocked his head from side to side as he pondered. "Following wheel tracks to Red Creek was my only good idea, so they could have retraced my steps. That'd take them to Delano Metz's house in Dead Man's Canyon."

She nodded and moved the wagon off through town and then toward the canyon. Her determination and the feeling that they were making progress cheered Bradley enough for him to sit up straight in the wagon.

His renewed vigor sustained him only until the canyon entrance became visible. So, with a weary feeling weighing down on him like a heavy blanket, he called to her and, when that failed to get her attention, he shuffled across the wagon and tapped her shoulder.

"What's wrong now?" she asked.

"I've had enough activity for today," he said. "Can we postpone seeing Delano until tomorrow?"

"We can't. We have to act quickly. All you've done is rest in the back of the wagon while I've done all the hard work."

"I don't feel good."

"You shouldn't. You've had two oper-
ations." She released a hand from the reins
to feel his forehead. "You're fine, and you
won't get better lying around in your bed."

"In that case I'll get better lying here,"
Bradley said before sliding to the left to lie
on his side.

He tucked his head down close to the side
of the wagon where he could enjoy some
shade and he let the rhythm of the trundling
wheels lull him to sleep. He must have
dozed as the next he knew the wagon had
stopped and Mary was kneeling on the seat
beside him.

When she'd gotten his attention, she
pointed so Bradley levered himself up to a
sitting position, pleasingly using his left
hand without thinking. They'd moved on
into Dead Man's Canyon, but he couldn't
work out what had concerned her until he
raised his head. Overhead, buzzards were
circling.

THIRTEEN

"Don't do this," Rattigan said.

He raised his hands and backed away for a pace now that he and Warner had done Thornton's bidding by scraping out graves for the dead marshal and for themselves. Thornton had been supervising their excavations and he shook his head before he raised his gun, but Orville came over while beckoning Thornton to hold his fire.

"You have one chance," Orville said with a smirk that promised his offer wouldn't be a good one. "Where did Corbin hide the silver?"

Warner caught Rattigan's eye, letting him know that if he had a ruse in mind, now was the time to employ it, so Rattigan thought quickly.

"Finding the silver and avoiding Corbin, if

he's alive, is only half your problems. While you were searching for Corbin's grave, the marshal found out that Victor got here first. He'll be angry we haven't found him."

The revelation made Thornton grin, but Orville winced and gestured with the gun, indicating that Rattigan and Warner should walk on ahead.

"Show me where he saw him," he said.

"They're trying to buy time and Victor won't cause us no problems," Thornton said. "Let me finish them off now."

"You're a railroad man, but I'm not and I'm in charge. I say what we do with them."

Thornton narrowed his eyes, seeming as if he'd defy him until he gave a sharp nod. Although, when Rattigan and Warner moved away, he considered the rest of the men as he clearly weighed up how many of them sided with Victor.

When they reached the edge of town and nobody was willing to venture beyond the buildings, Rattigan surmised that Thornton was in the minority. As the two men walked toward the wash, an unsettling feeling of vulnerability made Rattigan's heart quicken.

Every few steps he lowered himself so that he walked doubled over and then crouched down. By the time they were approaching the lip of the wash, they were snaking across the ground on knees and elbows.

Warner pointed at footprints ten yards ahead. Rattigan followed their path until they disappeared over the lip of the wash thirty yards ahead, so he directed Warner to stop. Then he crawled sideways seeking to gain a different angle on the scene ahead.

Slowly, the opposite side of the wash revealed itself as being steep-sided with loose scree covering half the height. The base and then the near side became visible. A gunshot broke the silence.

Rattigan jerked around on the spot seeking its source while Warner did the same. Warner turned to the lip of the wash where the footprints had led, but Rattigan faced the town. A second shot tore out.

This time Orville and the others moved within a building fifty yards away. Clearly, Victor had come looking for them before they'd sought him out. He got Warner's attention with a wave so Warner was lying on his side and facing the town when Victor and another man came out from a low building and ran toward the wash.

They hammered gunfire and Rattigan could do nothing other than to dive to the ground where he burrowed down into the dirt, seeking any available cover with his arms over his head. He heard only footfalls until Warner murmured in alarm.

When he raised his head Victor and the man had hunkered down beside Warner. Then, to Rattigan's surprise, from the town Orville hammered an accurate and deadly shot into the man's chest that made him stand up straight before he flopped down to lie over the edge of the wash.

Victor roared in defiance and in a coordinated move five men came over the lip of the wash to either side of him. They all had guns brandished and while they advanced, they peppered lead at the town forcing Orville and the rest of the prisoners to dive into cover.

Then a volley of gunshots rattled as Orville fought back. One of Victor's men keeled over clutching his neck, but then a cry of triumph sounded. Thornton had shown where his loyalties lay.

He was standing over Orville, who was lying propped up against a wall with his head resting on his bloodied chest. Then he toppled over. The sight made one of the prisoners run for safety.

He vaulted over the short wall he'd been hiding behind and with his head down he ran away from Thornton. Unfortunately, that moved him toward Victor's men and as one they fired.

He covered five paces before he threw up his hands and plowed face first into the dirt holding his chest. He arched his back and flopped down to lie still. This made the rest of the prisoners stay where they'd gone to ground while Thornton stood guard on the edge of town.

"Now it's time to repay you for assaulting me in Bear Rock," Victor called, turning his gun on Rattigan.

"That was an accident," Rattigan said. He had no hope of clemency, but as keeping Victor talking was the only way to delay the inevitable, he babbled an explanation as he shuffled toward him. "As you'd lost our silver, I went to your office to steal money. All I found was documents so I fled."

"What did you do with them?"

Rattigan didn't think that bargaining for information would work so he shook his head.

"They looked worthless so I threw them in the trash behind the Sagebrush saloon. Then I went back to see what else I could steal and I got the drop on you."

Victor flinched as gunfire erupted in the town, but he hadn't been the target. Thornton had decided to eliminate the rest of the prisoners. He'd already mowed down two men and the only surviving prisoner aside from Warner and Rattigan was jerking from side to side in confusion as to which direction would give him the best chance.

Then he turned on his heel and ran for the town, but unfortunately that took him toward Thornton, who shot at him. His shot slew wide and by the time he was ready to fire again, the man ran into him.

Both men tussled and then fell, landing on their sides and facing each other. Thornton kept hold of his weapon and he loosed off an involuntary shot that made his opponent fall away. Then he rolled to his feet and gestured triumphantly to Victor, who nodded and then turned back to Rattigan.

"Shoot us, and you'll never find Corbin," Rattigan said with as much defiance as he could muster.

"You know nothing," Victor said and snorted a laugh. "You've been scrabbling around in the dirt here without success."

"Except we know more than you do. For a start, Corbin never went to the dry creek."

Victor narrowed his eyes, this taunt appearing to annoy him more than Rattigan had expected.

"Your only chance is to show me Corbin's body." Victor flashed a thin smile. "You have one minute."

Rattigan didn't believe Victor would honor

his offer, but as he didn't have a choice, he spread his hands.

"You know I can't show you his body in a minute." Rattigan raised his chin. "Because Corbin's not here and he's not dead."

This proved to be the right thing to say as Victor winced, appearing as close to accepting defeat as he'd ever seen.

"I always suspected your idiot brother couldn't have defeated Corbin, so take me to him."

Buying time with a poor guess would anger Victor even more, so Rattigan sifted through the information he'd gathered about Corbin. He had learned little, but his conversations with Delano Metz felt as if they were the only times he'd heard the truth.

Delano had said he'd find his brother using the simplest means and, as far as Rattigan was concerned, the simplest way to find someone was to stay where you were and let them find you. He gestured back along the route they'd taken to get here.

"I'll take you to him," he said.

FOURTEEN

The buzzards' activities couldn't hide the fact that the dead men had been shot.

"These men have to be the merchants who found you," Mary said.

"I agree, although it's less certain who found them," Bradley said from the back of the wagon.

Mary kneeled beside the bodies and murmured a prayer, while Bradley turned to the boulders that marked the entrance to Dead Man's Canyon where Corbin had alighted on the way to Bear Rock. This observation reinforced his view that his quest would end where it had begun at Delano's house.

When they moved on, Mary sat hunched over on the seat and her expression was more troubled than he'd ever seen her show before. Even when he drew his gun and laid it on his lap, she only muttered in disapproval. She approached Delano's house from the side and pulled up between the house and the barn.

"I'll talk with Delano," she said while leaning forward. "You play with your gun and try not to hurt any rocks."

He shook his head. "I know you're a nun and you don't need protection, but if Delano's in there, he probably killed those two merchants. I'll go."

"You won't," she said.

She appeared ready to say more, but then she jumped down from the seat, deducing correctly that moving quickly would defeat him with greater ease than words.

"Be careful," Bradley called after her as he struggled to drag himself across the base of the wagon.

She stopped, making him think that his first kind words had surprised her, but she was looking beyond the house at a grave. A man was tied to a stake that lay over the hole, although who he was and whether he was dead or alive, Bradley couldn't tell. With the sight rooting Mary to the spot, Bradley had enough time to clamber out of the wagon and shuffle on to join her.

"You won't stop me from helping that man," she said.

"I wouldn't try, but. . . ." Bradley trailed off as the door swung open.

He had expected Delano to emerge, but to his surprise Corbin paced out, alive and well and with his gun already aimed at him. Bradley scrambled to raise his gun, but he fumbled over the unfamiliar movement and he'd yet to sight his target when Corbin fired, slicing a slug into the dirt a foot before Bradley's right boot.

"Drop your gun, or the next shot takes you between the eyes," Corbin said.

"Who are you?" Mary demanded, as Bradley opened his hand and raised his left arm.

"That's Corbin Metz," Bradley said.

"I was addressing him not you." Mary took a pace toward Corbin, seemingly oblivious to the gun he'd aimed at them. "He can also tell me who's lying over that grave."

Corbin turned to the grave and chuckled. "That's my brother Delano, although right now he's somewhat confused about his identity."

* * *

"I'm Corbin Metz," the man said. "I'm an evil gunslinger. I shoot up innocent men. I steal silver. I desecrate graves."

While he repeated his litany, he strained against his bonds, as he had done throughout the long day. He hoped he could drag himself free of the ropes and curl up in the grave, the only place a man like him deserved to be.

The fact he was evil was bad enough, but finding out his brother wasn't a decent man either had destroyed his last vestige of hope. Even worse, the memories that his brother had helped him rekindle had grown and he could now remember more.

All of it was bad. After his brother had left

him the first time, he had dug up this grave and extracted a coffin full of silver. He had been angry and he'd reburied the silver. Later, two men had brought his brother back.

His brother had demanded that he return the silver and when he'd refused, a fight had ensued. He had been hit on the head and his brother had chased the two men off. Confused and disorientated, he had fled with them.

His brother had pursued them and, in an ambush, he had killed the other two men while bringing down his horse. Then his brother had demanded again to know what he'd done with the silver, but he had passed out.

Later, he'd come to with his memory in so many tatters that only now could he reassemble some of his past. Even so, he couldn't remember all the bad things his brother had said he'd done, but he figured he'd remember them soon, if he wasn't lucky and death claimed him first.

He strained again, jutting his chest and

head down to the grave that he wanted to lie in for eternity. To his surprise, a creak sounded. Then the stake snapped and he jerked down for a foot before he halted.

He dangled, trapped within the entangling rope until, with another crack, he went clattering down into the bottom of the grave. He lay on his chest with the two halves of the broken stake lying on his back and the rope spread loosely around him.

He was so relieved he hugged the dirt, enjoying the coolness, but his relief was short-lived. The terrible truth about the man he was weighed down on him. So he clawed at the sides of the hole, seeking to drag earth over his body and hasten the end.

He was no gopher and he struggled to loosen the hard dirt. So he rolled over on to his back and faced the rectangle of light. The sky was now a twilight, blood red.

"I'm Corbin Metz," he said. "I'm an evil man."

The declaration made his heart race and a kernel of anger grew in his black soul. He nurtured it and let it grow until with a burst of energy he fought his way out from the rope and tossed the broken parts of the stake aside.

He came bounding out from the grave and stood on the side gasping in his breath. Every bone ached, but his head no longer troubled him giving him greater clarity than he could ever remember.

"My brother's an evil man, too," he said.

He chuckled, imagining the revenge he could enact on him to repay the beatings. Images came to him of the atrocities he could commit, as he enjoyed the power that came when he accepted no limits.

For that revenge, he needed a weapon. He didn't have one, but for a man as devious as he was, that was no problem. He slapped a hand on the bottom half of the pointed stake, hoisted it off the ground and held it at chest level. Then he set off for the house with his gait determined, the stake aimed forward and a twisted smile on his lips.

* * *

"I have duties to perform," Mary declared. "They don't include sitting around in your house all night."

Bradley winced, expecting swift retribution, but Corbin merely shrugged. He had brought them into the house, consisting of a single room furnished with only a table and two chairs along with a cot in the corner.

Throughout the afternoon, he had considered them earnestly, his silence seemingly designed to encourage them to talk, but Bradley hadn't wanted to risk engaging him in conversation and hasten the end.

Instead, he'd sat propped up against the side wall trying to stay awake while wishing he was back in the mission enjoying his bed and suffering Mary's disapproving looks. For her part, Mary had directed her ire at Corbin, which he had ignored with ease.

"You can leave when I have the answers I need," Corbin said.

"You'll only get your answers after you put down your gun."

Bradley groaned, imagining the bad direction this stand-off would now take.

"I'll put down my gun *after* I have my answers."

Mary pointed at the window where twilight was shrouding the shutters with the last light of the day.

"I told Deputy Crane in Bear Rock where I was going, so this can only turn out badly for you."

Bradley's eyelids had been drooping, but he snapped his eyes open in surprise when Mary lied. Corbin had a pained expression that Bradley had seen often recently.

"What must I do to stop you prattling on?"

"Let me tend to your brother. He'll need aid after being tied to that stake all afternoon."

"I can't relent when he's close to telling me what I need to know."

"Which is?"

Corbin sighed before he replied with the weary air of a man who had been dragged into a conversation that he didn't know how to end.

"After the raid in Bear Rock I buried the silver here. When I moved on, Delano dug it up and reburied it. So when he tells me where, everyone can go."

"You won't resolve your troubles by making your brother suffer." Mary snorted. "If you won't let me go to him, bring him here."

"Delano's not suffering." Corbin licked his lips and laughed. "He thinks he's me."

For once Mary struggled to find a reply, but as Bradley reckoned that when she did, it wouldn't help the situation, he spoke up for the first time since they'd been taken prisoner.

"The last time I saw Delano he thought you were innocent," he said with a hand held to his head to support it. "Why would he now make such a ridiculous claim?"

Corbin tapped his temple. "He lost his memory. I've been helping him get it back so he can tell me what he did with the silver. I reckoned a few hints that he's not the decent man he thinks he is might persuade him to talk."

"Doing that to your own brother when he only wanted to help you is worse than anything else you've ever done."

Corbin grunted with anger and walked across the room to stand over Bradley.

"Perhaps it is, but that only reminds me that back in Red Creek, you tried to kill me for the bounty."

Bradley raised his chin with defiance. "Do what you want with me, but let her go."

This offer made Mary get to her feet and gesture at Corbin.

"I'm not leaving without him, and I'm not going without you letting me help your brother," she said.

"Any more demands?" Corbin asked, raising an incredulous eyebrow.

"Something to eat and drink would be welcome."

Corbin winced, so Bradley gave an understanding frown. Then, with an aggrieved wave of the hand, Corbin headed to the door.

"I'll bring him here," he said. "Perhaps seeing what happened to the last man to defy me will help his memory return."

"Be quick about it," Mary called after him

while shooing him away.

Her comment made Corbin snarl as he threw open the door, but then he did a double-take. From his position at the side of the room, Bradley couldn't work out what had surprised him so his first inkling of what was outside came when an inhuman howl of anguish sounded.

Then Delano came bounding in, no longer looking the assured man he had been when he'd met him in the Sagebrush saloon. His eyes were manic and his clothes were bloody and ragged.

Clutched under an arm was a pointed stake, which he pressed to Corbin's chest and then drove on. His speed made Corbin back away with his arms flailing, but he couldn't move fast enough to avoid the stake that jabbed into his chest.

Corbin tumbled over on to his back and, with the stake caught up in his clothing, Delano went down with him. A wet crunching noise sounded making Mary wince. When Delano rolled off his brother, Bradley winced, too. The stake had driven down through Corbin's chest, transfixing him to the floor.

"I only wanted the silver and to kill Victor," Corbin murmured, blood bubbling on his lips. "I'd have let you go."

"I don't care," Delano said, getting to his knees. "I'm an evil man. You said so."

Corbin raised a hand to the stake, but his strength gave out and his head flopped to the side. Delano poked his ribs, his tense expression defying Corbin to fight back, but he lay still, the six inch wide stake that pinned him to the floor confirming that this time he was dead.

Delano picked up Corbin's gun. As he hefted it, Bradley crawled toward him, but Delano raised a hand and a few moments later Bradley heard what had interested him. Outside, hoofbeats were approaching. Mary had been moving to kneel beside Corbin, but she headed to the window.

"It's Victor Greystone and his heathen men," she reported as the riders drew up. She turned to Bradley. "You explain the truth to Delano while I deal with him."

"You won't," Bradley said.

Mary shook a finger at him in a way that said he was in no fit state to confront anyone, but Delano made the first move and leaped to his feet with Corbin's gun held aloft.

"I'll take him on," he proclaimed. "I'll take them all on. I'm Corbin Metz and I run from no man."

"You're not Corbin," Mary said, speaking slowly as she walked toward him. "Your brother treated you badly and you're confused."

"Stay away. I won't hesitate to kill a nun." Delano turned to the door. "Neither will I hesitate before I take on these men."

He brushed past Mary on his way to the door, which he threw open to stand defiantly in the doorway.

"Don't," Bradley said from the floor. "You're no gunslinger."

Delano shook his head and took a pace forward, his gun swinging down to pick out the men outside. He was as slow to take aim as Bradley had expected and he'd yet to sight anyone when gunfire tore out.

A few seconds later he came staggering back into the house with the gun falling from his grasp and his chest holed. His expression was one of open-mouthed surprise, which turned to a pained grimace when another burst of gunfire blasted into his back making him topple over sideways.

"It seems I'm not," he said.

As he'd fallen away from the doorway, Bradley crawled across the floor to his side.

"You can't die not knowing the truth," he said. "You're not the outlaw Corbin. You're Delano, a decent man."

Delano nodded, his eyes glazing. "I am. I remember. I remember it all. I. . . ."

Delano exhaled a long breath and Bradley thought he wouldn't speak again, but then with his eyes closing he beckoned him to come closer using a bent finger. Bradley leaned over him and Delano whispered to him, his voice a light breeze that calmed and then silenced.

"What did he say?" Mary asked from the other side of the door.

Bradley ignored her as the gun Delano had dropped in the doorway was three yards away and even in his weak state, he reckoned he could reach it. He took a deep breath and prepared to take his chances, but before he could move, Victor stepped into the doorway and slammed a heavy boot down on the gun.

He sneered at Delano and then Bradley with equal contempt before turning to the skewered Corbin. A wide smile appeared.

"So it's over," he declared. Then he gestured at the men outside. "Put them all in here and then we'll burn this place to the ground."

FIFTEEN

Thornton moved in and grabbed Rattigan from behind. Rattigan struggled and tried to buck him, but his captor had gathered a firm grip. With Rattigan being seized first, Warner had a few seconds' warning and he used his temporary freedom to run.

He turned away from the house, but this moved him toward the rest of Victor's men, who were closing in on the door. Three men swooped in and secured him leaving Victor's remaining man to busy himself with lighting a brand.

Victor had spared their lives until he'd confirmed Rattigan's guess about Corbin. Victor's gleeful expression as he'd ordered them to be put in the building along with the scene in the house extinguished all his hope.

Corbin was lying dead on the floor behind his shot-up brother. Sister Mary was saying prayers over Delano, while Bradley was sitting on the floor, his pained expression showing he was using all his strength just to stay upright.

Bradley registered his presence with a wan shrug before he lowered his head to rest his chin on his chest. Victor stopped outside the doorway and he directed a triumphant look at Rattigan before Thornton threw Rattigan into the house.

Rattigan had to veer away to avoid Delano and the nun, and his quick motion made him slip. He went to one knee where he faced the door, aiming to leap to his feet and make a last bid for freedom, but Warner was being dragged in after him.

Warner fought back using berserk strength that kept his three captors occupied. When they reached the doorway, the constricted space forced one man to release him and, with only two men holding him, Warner tore himself free.

He still ended up tumbling head over

heels into the house. As this result was what they had been trying to achieve, his captors laughed and turned away. They had taken two steps away when one of the men slapped a hand to his holster and turned quickly.

He found himself facing a smiling Warner with that man's gun clutched low. Warner fired and blasted a slug up into the unarmed man's chest making him drop. Then Warner gained his feet and took on the other two men in the doorway.

He fired again, but this time his shot sliced wide of its target, giving the other two men enough time to get their wits about them. Two simultaneous gunshots rang out and both slugs hammered into Warner's chest making him hunch over.

Warner staggered backward for two paces before with a defiant shake of the head he righted himself and raised his gun. They shot at him again, the slugs slicing into his chest, but not before he fired again, downing one of his opponents before he keeled over on to his back and then became still.

To the side of the doorway, Rattigan judged he couldn't cover the ten feet to claim Warner's gun before one of the men outside shot him. Bradley was on his knees, but he was holding his left arm across his chest with a defensive posture that said he didn't reckon he had the strength to reach it.

Bradley set off anyhow. He'd crawled on for only a few feet when Victor spoke up from outside and out of Rattigan's view.

"You won't lay a finger on that gun," he said. "As I told you, no man has ever drawn a gun on me twice."

Bradley gritted his teeth and crawled on, encouraging Victor to move into the doorway. His shadow flickered presumably as one of his men had now lit a brand. The sight made Mary move calmly toward him.

"There's been enough bloodshed today," she declared. "You'll now end this."

"Which is what I'm doing."

The shadow moved as Victor took the lighted brand. The fire made Mary balk so Victor stepped into the house. He sported an eager grin as he thrust the flames toward her, which made her back away and her distress even made Bradley stop dragging himself forward.

Rattigan accepted he had to try to reach the gun. He stood up and edged forward while on the other side of the doorway Victor advanced on Mary. He reckoned it'd take two long paces and a dive to reach the gun, but with the doorway coming into view, a better option presented itself of the gun that Delano had dropped.

Victor had walked past it so in a quick decision he took a step to the side and leaped. As he fell, Thornton and another man moved in the doorway. He hit the floor on his side beside the gun and gathered it up, his momentum barreling him through the doorway where he fortuitously upended Thornton before he came to rest outside on his knees.

He jerked the gun toward the other man, who was turning at the hip to follow his progress and the two men faced each other a moment before Rattigan fired. From only a few feet away, his gunshot tore into the man's chest making him stand up straight before he ripped a second shot into him a foot lower.

With a hand rising to his chest, the man staggered backward and toppled through the doorway. With Thornton having fallen inside, Rattigan rose to his feet and ran for the wall where he swung around, searching for his next target.

A slug tore into the wall beside his right arm, giving him a clue that the gunman was straight ahead, but he wasn't visible. Feeling exposed, he crouched and the movement saved him from a shot that sliced into the wall where his head had been.

Better still, the gunman revealed that he was in the barn, having taken cover behind a stack of old crates. Rattigan trained his gun above the crates and the moment the man bobbed up again, he fired.

His shot clipped wood and it only suc-ceeded in making the man drop down out of view. Rattigan moved away from the wall and, sure enough, when the man rose up again, he had aimed at the wall and he used valuable moments jerking his gun to the side.

Before he could get Rattigan in his sights, Rattigan fired. He winged the shooter's shoulder making him stumble and the man stayed in view for long enough for Rattigan to hammer a second shot into his stomach making him drop.

Behind him in the house Mary shouted in alarm making Rattigan turn. As his six-shooter held a maximum of one bullet, he aimed at the doorway while he hurried toward the nearest fallen man.

He had yet to reach him when Thornton stepped into the doorway. Rattigan fired, but only a click sounded so with a smirk on his lips Thornton took careful aim at his chest. Rattigan hurled the weapon at him.

That at least made Thornton cringe away, but the moment it'd clattered through the door, he aimed again at him. A gunshot cracked making Rattigan tense until Thornton flinched and reached for his back.

Then he dropped to his knees and toppled forward into the dirt to reveal Bradley through the doorway. His brother had dragged himself to Warner's body and claimed his gun, but it had been a struggle to fire, as he'd had to lean on Warner's chest to keep the gun steady.

So Rattigan moved quickly. He hurried on to Thornton and claimed his gun. Then he ran into the house keeping low. Flames were flickering and throwing up shadows, so he was able to pick out Victor quickly, but he stayed his fire.

Victor had now seized Mary and he was holding her from behind with his gun pressed against her temple. To their side, he'd dropped the brand on the cot and flames were scooting up the wall.

"We've got two guns on you, Victor," Rattigan said. "It's time to give up."

Victor raised his chin. "Your brother doesn't have the strength to keep his gun steady. So it's between you and me, and you won't let me shoot her."

Bradley swayed as his strength gave out, and the flames were rising, filling the ceiling space with smoke as the shingles caught alight.

"You men will stop arguing and do what I say," Mary said.

Victor swung her around to place her between him and Rattigan, so that he could use her as a shield when he walked to the door.

"Keep quiet, or I'll end your prattle now," he said.

While making his last demand he coughed and, with the fire forcing them to resolve their stand-off quickly, Rattigan stepped to the side to block Victor's route to the door.

"I won't be silent for no man," Mary said. She turned to Bradley. "You'll do as I've told you to and put down that gun."

"I can't," Bradley said, his voice weak. "He'll kill you."

She gestured at Victor's gun. "That situation is no worse than the current one. Have faith. The way of the gun won't resolve anything."

Bradley shocked Rattigan by nodding. His capitulation made Victor drag Mary closer, seemingly expecting subterfuge, but he raised his eyebrows in surprise when Bradley moved his gun to the side to aim at his brother.

"What are you doing, Bradley?" Rattigan demanded.

"I'm doing what she said," Bradley said. "I'm taking the only option that'll save her life and yours."

The flames had now gained a decisive hold of the roof in the corner.

"Are you saying we should let Victor walk out of here with a hostage?"

"No." Bradley centered his gun on Rattigan's chest. "I'm saying we should do what Mary says and throw down our guns. Then we'll leave before this place burns down."

As Mary nodded, Rattigan shook his head.

"I don't know what nonsense that nun's been telling you, but if we do that, Victor will kill us all."

"He won't, because I can give him the one thing he wants."

"Explain," Victor said, taking a pace toward the door.

"I'll tell Deputy Crane I helped Corbin steal the silver. I'll say I helped him evade capture and that he admitted he killed Marshal Dagwood. In short, I'll take the blame for everything and let you walk away from this without repercussions."

Victor smiled. "Get your brother to join you in throwing down your gun and you have a deal."

Bradley firmed his gun hand, his teeth gritted with effort, making Rattigan frown, but then a burning ember drifted down between them. That heralded a plume of smoke that spread down and across the room, making him back away to avoid it.

"All right, I'll trust you," he said.

He dropped the gun at his feet and a moment later Bradley threw his gun away before flopping down to lie on his back. Victor rocked from foot to foot, clearly still anticipating deception. Then the plume of smoke reached him making him cough uncontrollably.

"Deal," he managed to bleat between coughs. Then he shoved Mary on toward the door.

Rattigan hurried to Bradley's side. He helped him to a sitting position and Bradley placed his left arm around his shoulder before he raised him to his feet. Victor and Mary had now gone through the door so, as they shuffled after them, he leaned toward Bradley.

"I hope you know what you're doing," he said.

"I hope so, too," Bradley said as he turned his head from the billowing smoke. "I figured there was only one way we could beat Victor, and that was to let him win."

SIXTEEN

"Is that the truth?" Deputy Crane asked when Bradley had finished his testimony.

It was now around midnight after Mary had returned to Bear Rock to fetch Crane along with two deputies. Bradley sat on the ground inside the barn with his back resting against the wall while Rattigan and Mary stood in the doorway, shaking their heads.

"I did it all," Bradley said and lowered his head.

Crane frowned. His willingness to believe Bradley's story had been low after being told that Marshal Bishop had been killed.

"What happened to the silver?"

Bradley gave a tense smile. "Before he died Delano told me he buried it in the same place Corbin did, in their parents' grave."

"We can see the open grave over there," Mary said before Crane could reply, making him turn to her. "The silver's not there."

"That was Delano's ruse. He dug down and buried it even deeper, figuring Corbin wouldn't look in the same place where he'd buried it."

Crane and Mary both shrugged before with a sigh Crane turned to the door.

"So now I guess I've got no choice but to check out your story," he said. "If it's true, it'll help you, but I reckon either way you'll be in a cell for a long time."

"For his crimes, he should never leave it," Victor said, moving to stand alongside Crane. "But I promised you and Marshal Bishop that I'd help you bring Marshal Dagwood's killer to justice. I'm pleased that tonight we can finally end this matter."

"I'm obliged for your unwavering support," Crane said. "After this, I'll need your help again to move Bear Rock forward."

"It'll be a pleasure." Victor beamed at Bradley. "I'll start by joining you and the other deputies in digging up the silver."

Crane nodded and ushered everyone to leave the barn. Victor directed a triumphant smirk at Rattigan and Mary before he left them, but Mary didn't move.

"You shouldn't stay here with the prisoner," Crane said.

"When your job ends, mine begins," Mary declared. "I'll talk to Bradley. When you have your silver, he may have more information for you."

Crane frowned, but before he had a chance to reject her offer, Victor started walking purposefully away from the barn. So he gathered his two deputies and they hurried past the still smoldering house to the burial plot. Nobody spoke until Crane and Victor were standing on either side of the grave and the deputies had begun digging.

"You can't do this," Rattigan said, heading into the barn.

Bradley lay on his back and placed his left arm over his face, so Mary joined Rattigan in standing over him.

"Listen to your brother," she said. "You

can't do this."

"Crane says your mission will get the bounty on Corbin's head," Bradley said wearily. "So this is the right way."

"I'm not concerned about the money. I am concerned about you and your lies. I wanted you to reject the gun to become a better person, but this foolish gesture is worse."

"I made a promise to Victor to save your life." Bradley raised his arm. "I have to keep it."

"I'm glad you listened to me, but keeping a promise made to that man, and which lets him remain free, is wrong. I'd sooner have died than let this happen."

"I'll be glad when you admit I can be right sometimes." Bradley laughed when Mary shook her head. "I'm keeping my promise because it's the only way I can defeat Victor."

"How?" she asked, spreading her hands.

Bradley raised himself on to an elbow and held his head to one side as if listening. He nodded and gestured for Rattigan to help him to his feet.

"Patience," Bradley said. "We'll get to see how in a moment."

With Rattigan holding a hand under his armpit and with Mary at his side, they trudged to the doorway. The deputies had dug down quickly and by moonlight they were visible only down to their waists. Then a cry of triumph sounded and one deputy clambered out of the hole to kneel on the ground while the other deputy dropped down to disappear from view.

"It looks like they've found our silver, but how will that help defeat Victor?" Rattigan said.

Bradley gripped Rattigan's arm and then moved away to stand alone.

"Because before he died Delano enjoyed a brief moment of clarity. He told me that Corbin had etched an inscription on the coffin that he'd hidden in when we brought him into town."

"I know. We saw the plaque with the initials KD."

"Except nobody saw the full inscription. It says that KD was killed by VG, and the silver is lying below that coffin."

Mary shrugged. "If Deputy Crane sees the inscription, it'll shake Victor up, but not enough to prove he did it and to keep you out of jail."

Bradley leaned toward her. "Except what's lying among the silver will. That's where Delano put the documents he stole from the railroad office."

Bradley gestured at Rattigan for him to complete the story.

"They detail the bribes Victor paid along with his activities in Bear Rock," Rattigan said, turning to Mary, "and perhaps a whole lot more things that'll incriminate him."

"If that doesn't do more than merely rattle him, I'll tell the truth," Bradley said. "I guess we'll find out his response in the next few minutes."

Rattigan nodded and then beckoned for Bradley and Mary to stay by the barn. He moved away while craning his neck as he sought out Victor's and Crane's reactions. Victor appeared confident as he let the deputies work out how to get the heavy silver out of the hole.

First, they dumped the coffin on the ground, but with the silver in the hole attracting everyone's attention, nobody looked at the lid. Rattigan moved on to join Crane, and the deputy raised a hand, warning him to stay back.

So he sat on the coffin lid and turned to the hole. There appeared to be enough silver below to account for everything they'd lost, but that didn't interest him as much as the small folded sack lying amid the silver.

He rose up and then stood over the coffin. He jerked backward and grunted, as if he'd been surprised by what he'd seen, even though so much dirt covered the lid in the moonlight he couldn't confirm the inscription said what Bradley claimed it did.

"What does that say?" he asked, pointing at the lid.

Crane shrugged, but Victor must have been already concerned as he stomped around the hole and barged Rattigan aside. Then he turned around to stand in front of the coffin.

"You need to stay over there with your good-for-nothing brother," he said, gesturing at the barn.

"I will, but I just thought the inscription on the lid said something interesting."

Rattigan moved to the side, making Victor block his way.

"It says nothing that should concern you."

Rattigan dismissed the matter with a shrug and turned his back on Victor, but his comments had done enough to gather Crane's interest. He moved around the hole forcing Victor to turn to him.

With neither man paying him attention, Rattigan stood over the hole. The deputies were clearing away the dirt at each end so he jumped down into the middle and claimed the sack before turning back.

"So what does it say?" Crane asked.

"I can't read it by moonlight, but maybe you'll have more luck," Victor said.

Victor stepped back with a smirk on his face and when Crane moved to bend over the lid, he edged his hand toward his holster, but Crane shrugged, accepting he couldn't read it.

"I thought that it said something about Marshal Ken Dagwood being killed by Victor Greystone," Rattigan said from the hole.

"Lies," Victor said.

Rattigan raised the sack. "I assume that what's in this sack is more lies, or maybe it's just what Delano stole from your office."

Victor's eyes flared as he noticed the sack for the first time. He held out his left hand.

"If that's my property, hand it over."

"I reckon Crane will be more interested in reading what's in here first."

"I sure will," Crane said as Victor glowered at Rattigan.

The deputy thrust out a hand for the sack, but Victor snarled, seemingly dismissing trying to talk his way out of the situation. Then he pushed Crane aside with one hand while he scrambled for his gun with the other hand.

Being unarmed, Rattigan did the only thing he could do and dropped to his knees. The deputies on either side of him reacted slowly and before they could touch leather,

Victor splayed gunfire across their chests, making them both fall backward to lie sprawled over the edge of the hole.

Crane had enough time to draw his gun, but Victor twisted at the hip and before the lawman could fire Victor slammed a high shot into his chest that dropped him. In a moment Victor jerked back to face the kneeling Rattigan.

"You'll never get away with shooting up all these lawmen," Rattigan said.

"I got away with killing Marshal Dagwood," Victor said. "The rest shouldn't cause me no problem."

Victor firmed his gun hand making Rattigan tense, but then a sly smile spread across Victor's face and he moved around to stand on the other side of coffin. Rattigan moved to clamber out of the hole, but Victor kicked the coffin toward him, barring his way.

Over by the barn Bradley was making his slow and pained way toward them while Mary trotted along beside him with an arm raised as she urged him to return to the barn. Bradley was clearly ignoring her, but he wouldn't reach them for at least another minute and then Rattigan doubted his brother would be in a fit enough state to help him.

Victor's confident smirk suggested he was of the same mind. He pointed at the coffin.

"You want me to get in there?" Rattigan asked.

"You bought the coffin into town and started this whole sorry situation," Victor said. "I reckon that's the right place for you to be when I end it."

Rattigan reached out of the hole and slapped a hand down on the lid. When he drew the lid away from the coffin, the lid slipped down into the hole and came to rest standing upright. The plaque caught the light showing him what Corbin had etched there.

Rattigan tapped the wood. "You won't keep this truth hidden forever."

"I'll fire down through the lid until those words are obliterated, along with you. Then, after I've disposed of your brother and his annoying friend, I'll burn the evidence in that sack in the remnants of the house fire."

Victor raised an eyebrow, giving Rattigan a chance to find fault in his plans, and Rattigan nodded as if he were considering, but only because his foot had nudged against the shovel that one of the deputies had been using. Then, with a shrug, he underhanded the sack to Victor.

Victor was only four feet away and he caught the sack one-handed, but Rattigan used the time to drop to one knee and root around for the shovel handle. It came to hand quickly and he rose up with it brandished before him.

With a snarl of anger Victor fired and a loud metallic noise sounded. Even as Rattigan realized the shovel blade had deflected the bullet, he launched the shovel at Victor. The shovel turned over in the air and for a moment Rattigan hoped the blade would slice into Victor's chest, but then it continued turning and the handle slammed into his shoulder.

The blow was still strong enough to knock

Victor backward so while he was floundering, Rattigan pressed down on the top of the lid and used the leverage to vault out of the hole. He had no other weapon to hand so he did the only thing he could do and gathered a firm hold of the lid.

His last sight of Victor before he raised the lid from the hole and placed it before his face was of him righting himself. Then, with the lid held before him as a shield, he charged at Victor.

He covered two paces before a shot rang out and he felt the lid kick, but he moved on and as he reached Victor, he thrust out the lid to arm's length. He slammed into him and, with his arms locked, he knocked him backward until Victor tumbled over on to his back.

Rattigan moved on for another step and then dropped down. He landed on top of Victor and pressed down on the lid, leaving Victor lying beneath the lid with his limbs splayed out like a massive bug crushed beneath a boot.

Victor tried to buck him, but Rattigan

resisted while feeling for Victor's gun arm. The gun was being brandished close to his shoulder and Victor was moving his gun hand freely. Rattigan was keeping his opponent pinned down and he didn't want to risk going for the gun for fear of relinquishing his only advantage.

But Victor must have worked out his exact location as the gun swung around to aim at his chest with unerring accuracy. Rattigan shifted his weight as he prepared to leap aside, but then the light level lowered a moment before a heavy boot came crunching down on Victor's wrist.

Victor managed to loose off a shot, but it flew wide. Bradley pressed down on the wrist making Victor screech in pain. Then the gun fell from his grasp. Mary was behind Bradley and while Bradley swooped on Victor's gun, she moved around the lid to stand over the hole.

"You appear to have Victor subdued this time," she declared. "Keep him there while I check on the lawmen."

When she kneeled beside Crane, Rattigan

and Bradley smiled at each other.

"You arrived just in time," Rattigan said.

"I may be missing a good hand, but I still have a good foot," Bradley said as he stood back to aim the gun down at Victor.

* * *

"I gather Deputy Crane will recover," Mary said when she arrived at the law office. "One other deputy has a good chance of surviving Victor's assault, too, but I'm afraid the other one died."

"It could have been worse, but at least everyone now knows what Victor did," Rattigan said.

Bradley frowned and Mary lowered her head for a moment confirming this was only a small crumb of comfort. It had taken them most of what was left of the night to end the situation.

Mary had returned to town to fetch help while the brothers had kept watch over their prisoner, but with two guns on him and while nursing a broken wrist, Victor hadn't given them any trouble. Victor was now in a cell while Bradley and Rattigan were sitting in the law office and waiting to tell their story to whoever would listen to them.

"I'll leave you now," Mary said. "I have matters to attend to that are more important than apprehending outlaws."

Both men nodded to her, but neither man spoke until she'd left them.

"Spending time with her has helped you, and in more ways than just tending your injuries," Rattigan said.

"I have to accept I can't sort out my problems by knocking people down no more," Bradley said, gesturing at his missing arm. "Mary was right that I have to find other solutions."

"I guess I learned to find other solutions, too." Rattigan frowned. "So what will you do after we've both told our stories?"

Bradley thought about this before he strained to sit up straight in his chair.

"I reckon I'll follow Mary back to the mission and rest up." Bradley sighed. "I never thought I'd say it, but once I feel better, I might stay on there. With Sister Mary in charge, those nuns are sure to attract trouble."

"In other words, you can't move on until she admits you've been right about something."

"There is that." Bradley frowned. "What about you?"

"The mine's silver is now safe, but the miners will still need supplies. So I'll complete my mission." He smiled. "With any luck, despite all the trouble I'll still have a job, so before long I'll be back this way."

"I'll look forward to it." Bradley returned the smile. "After a few months spent with Mary, I might even appreciate spending time with my brother again."

CLEARWATER JUSTICE

Scott Connor

For five long years Deputy Jim Lawson has wanted to find the man who murdered his brother Benny. So when prime suspect Tyler Coleman rides into Clearwater, Jim slaps him in jail. But almost immediately the only witness to the appalling crime turns up dead and the outlaw Luther Wade rides into town and vows to break Tyler out of jail by sundown.

Then Jim's investigation takes an unexpected twist when he finds evidence linking Benny's murder to the disappearance of the beguiling Zelma Hayden, the woman he had once hoped to marry.

Can Jim uncover the truth before the many guns lining up against him deliver their own justice?

CULBIN PRESS

Made in United States
North Haven, CT
06 January 2024

47124528R00129